'I see the truth is starting to dawn,' he m

'Were you really   ee
Leon's plans for   of
finding me a wife

'Oh, no.'

'Oh, yes. You, my dear Australian minx, are Leon's choice of bride for me.'

The cold irony in his voice struck her like a blow. 'Now, just a minute. Surely I have some say in this?'

Valerie Parv was a successful journalist and non-fiction writer until she began writing for Mills & Boon in 1982. Born in Shropshire, England, she grew up in Australia and now lives with her cartoonist husband and their cat—the office manager—in Sydney, New South Wales. She is a keen futurist, a *Star Trek* enthusiast, and her interests include travelling, restoring dolls' houses and entertaining friends. Writing romance novels affirms her belief in love and happy endings.

Recent titles by the same author:

A ROYAL
ROMANCE

BY
VALERIE PARV

MILLS & BOON

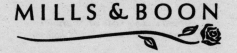

*First published in Great Britain 1996
Harlequin Mills & Boon Limited,
Eton House, 18-24 Paradise Road, Richmond, Surrey TW9 1SR*

© Valerie Parv 1996

ISBN 0 263 79941 7

*Set in Times Roman 11 on 12 pt.
02-9701-47170 C1*

*Printed and bound in Great Britain
by Mackays of Chatham PLC, Chatham*

CHAPTER ONE

THE palace had to be seen to be believed. Norah Kelsey gasped as her teenage companion led the way into yet another picturesque courtyard. 'Talay Rasada, will you please slow down so I can take this in? It's all so incredibly exotic.'

Talay laughed. 'No more exotic than your Australia was to me. We have nothing so adorable as your kangaroos balancing so sweetly on their long tails.'

Not so sweet if aroused, Norah couldn't help thinking. She didn't say it, preferring to let the teenager enjoy her illusions, as Norah herself relished the illusion of living in a fairytale. The reality was very different, as she well knew from her only previous visit to Sapphan. But that was in the past. For now she was content to enjoy seeing the island kingdom through the eyes of its youngest royal family member.

Talay squeezed her arm affectionately. 'I'm glad you travelled home with me, Norah.' Her hand went to her cheek. 'I was sure everyone would stare at me.'

'Well, now you know they don't,' Norah assured her charge briskly. 'So you needn't hide behind that hand anymore, or you'll rub off all our careful handiwork.'

Talay's hand slid down but she kept her head lowered as if to symbolically shield her damaged face. There was no real need. The special make-up Norah had designed for her completely camouflaged the surgical scars, which so concerned the teenager. Only the closest inspection would reveal a less than perfect complexion. 'You will keep practising with the make-up once you're back at school, won't you?' Norah asked.

Talay's look turned solemn. 'Of course, until the scars fade, which should be in a few months, the surgeon told me. He was pleased to hear you were coming with me. He says you're good for me.'

Norah's cheeks grew warm. 'Your grandfather deserves the credit. It was his idea,' she denied. 'He loves you very much.'

'I know. He's my best friend, next to you, of course.'

Talay couldn't know how much she flattered Norah. Leon Rasada was the elder statesman of the ruling house of Sapphan. Despite his formidable appearance, he was a wise and gentle man. From Talay, Norah knew Leon had been a tower of strength to his teenage grand daughter after her parents were killed in the plane crash that scarred Talay herself.

Setting aside his grief over losing his son and daughter-in-law, Leon had brought Talay to Australia for specialist treatment.

It was at the hospital that Norah first met the pair. She specialised in cosmetic therapy, helping youngsters like Talay to conceal their scars and enhance their best features. She was thrilled and humbled by the way Talay had blossomed under the programme.

Now, perched on the stone rim of a pool, Talay trailed long fingers through the cool water. 'You can stay here if you want to.'

Norah bit her lip. Agreeing to accompany Talay back to Sapphan, she had worried that the eventual parting would be a wrench for the teenager. 'We talked about this, Tal. You know I can only stay for a holiday. If I don't go back to Sydney I won't be able to open my own clinic someday, to help other girls like you.'

Talay pouted. 'You can open a clinic here. Lots of Sapphanese girls would benefit, and my uncle would be your patron if I asked him to.'

Which was precisely why Norah couldn't consider remaining. The last person she wanted to be indebted to was Talay's uncle, Philippe Rasada, ruler of Sapphan and soon to be crowned absolute monarch.

An involuntary shudder shook her at the thought of him. He was the reason she had resisted Leon's plea for her to accompany Talay, in spite of Norah's attachment to the young royal. It had taken all of Leon's considerable powers of persuasion to overcome Norah's reluctance. Even the huge fee he had offered her, which would go a long way towards realising her dream of opening her own clinic, hadn't decided her. Why had she agreed to come? She wasn't sure herself.

'It's a shame you can't stay for Uncle Philippe's coronation,' Talay said with the enthusiasm of a teenager for her favourite pop star. 'He'll make a dreamy king. Not that he isn't a spunky prince,' she added hastily, 'but as king he'll be perfect. If you could meet him you'd see for yourself.'

Finding that Philippe would be busy preparing for the coronation during Norah's visit had decided her. She wouldn't have come if there had been any chance of meeting him again, not after the last time. Her insides clenched involuntarily at the memory. 'I did meet your uncle once,' she admitted in carefully neutral tones.

Talay was instantly agog. 'You did? When?'

Norah held up a hand. 'It was only briefly at an official reception, and it was five years ago, so he's probably forgotten it. I was here on a modelling assignment, and the whole crew was invited to a palace reception.'

Talay grinned. 'I knew you were beautiful enough to be a model. Why did you give it up?'

'Lots of reasons.' The main one being Talay's precious Uncle Philippe. Playing on her looks, he'd called it, more accurately than even he knew. Norah had become a model in defiance of her parents, who valued intellect over all and were forever holding up Norah's brother, David, successful doctor, as their ideal.

They were horrified when she announced she was going into modelling, and even less pleased when her earnings had equalled her surgeon brother's in her first year. Unfortunately it was stultifying work, because she did possess a brain, in spite of her parents' misgivings. She just wasn't as academically inclined as David.

'What were you doing in Sapphan?' Talay asked, drawing her knees up and wrapping her nut-brown arms around them.

'Shooting a summer fashion catalogue using your gorgeous beaches as a backdrop,' Norah explained. 'In the fashion industry, summer clothes are photographed in the middle of winter to get the catalogues ready for the next season.'

Talay sighed. 'I wish I'd known you then. Was it very glamorous?'

Her mind flashed back five years. 'I thought so then.'

'But not any more?'

Norah shook her head. 'The rest of the crew was much more worldly than me, but I wanted to fit in, so I behaved badly, wore too much make-up and clothes I thought made me look more sophisticated. But they only made me look cheap.'

Talay looked dubious but Norah had long ago faced facts. After her family's indifference towards her, the crew had become a family of sorts, however unsuitable.

When Alain Montri, a minor royal and aide to the prince, became the crew's liaison with the palace, he had quickly singled Norah out for attention, which she was naive enough to encourage. He had believed she was as experienced as she pretended, and at first his attention had flattered her.

Then came the royal reception. She had been aware of the prince watching her with an expression of disdain, which so reminded her of her parents' attitude that she began to behave even more outrageously, not only with Alain but with several other men at the reception.

To her chagrin she found herself wondering what would happen if the prince asked her to dance, but he kept his distance. His dark, brooding air was so obviously critical of her that she became even more reckless as the night wore on.

Nevertheless it was hard to keep up an act that was so foreign to her nature, and finally she slipped out alone into the fragrant night air. She hadn't realised that Alain was waiting for her until he pounced, silencing her protests with passionate kisses as he half-dragged her into the seclusion of the shrubbery.

Then he had lowered her to the ground, her struggles futile. Heartbrokenly sure of the outcome, she had gone limp, on the verge of fainting, when there was a crash in the bushes and an eloquent stream of Sapphani language, which would probably have made her ears burn in translation.

At the sound, Alain had slipped off into the night, leaving her sobbing brokenly on the ground as she clutched her torn clothing around her.

She would never forget the expression of disgust on Philippe's face as he towered over her. 'Get up and cover yourself.'

Scrambling to her feet, she had made the attempt. Although the night was warm, she shivered with reaction. 'I'm so glad you came along, Your Highness.'

His dark eyebrows had arched disdainfully. 'I sincerely doubt it.'

The courtesies fled in the face of her shock. 'What?'

'I doubt whether you're glad I interrupted your pleasure. I understand that customs differ in your country, but as a visitor you might endeavour to respect local mores.'

The black eyes hammered home his message until she reeled back. 'You can't think I *wanted* this to happen?'

'What else am I to think? Your provocative clothes and your behaviour brand you as a temptress.'

'A temptress? It sounds positively medieval. I thought Sapphan was progressive.'

He shrugged as if her opinion was of no consequence. 'We are progressive in the things that matter.' His eyes narrowed. 'And traditional also in the things that matter.'

He had no idea that her would-be attacker was his precious aide. She could imagine the prince's response if she told him. It was her word against Alain Montri's, and she had no doubt who the prince would believe, especially as he had just made his opinion of her abundantly clear.

Instinctively she held herself taller, her model's height still only bringing her to the level of the prince's shoulder. He must be over two metres tall, but she refused to let him intimidate her, difficult though it was when she knew he held absolute power over his domain.

'I'm sorry you have such a poor opinion of me,' she said, knowing she sounded not the least bit apologetic, 'but my clothes and poses are as much a part of my job as ... as swords and epaulets are a part of yours, yet they're far from representative.'

She was referring to the prince's appearance at an official ceremony the day before, when he'd been dressed in an elaborate uniform and dress sword described by one of the photographers as 'straight out of *The Student Prince*.'

One side of his mouth twisted with a fleeting trace of amusement and his dark eyes sparked, momentarily softening his hawklike features. 'Touché,' he said, so softly that she wasn't sure she'd heard correctly. Then disapproval pulled his black brows together. 'None of which excuses this behaviour.' His gesture took in her disarranged clothing.

She lifted her chin, quailing inwardly as she met his unwavering black gaze. 'I have nothing more to say.'

'Not even a name, Miss Kelsey? No-one you want to blackmail with accusations of rape?'

'Your choice of words shows how much chance I have of being believed, so I prefer to remain silent.'

A grudging respect flickered in his assessing look. 'No wonder the unfortunate man ran off, if you responded as aggressively to him as to me.'

She gave a bitter half-smile. 'It's a bad habit of mine, defending myself when attacked.'

'So now you say he was attacking you?'

Annoyed, she tossed her head, her hair flying in a golden halo around her head. 'I don't *say* he was attacking me—he damned well was.'

His expression hardened again and his fingers snapped in front of her face. 'He? A name, Miss Kelsey, if you please.'

'You wouldn't believe me, any more than you believe I didn't invite his attention.'

'If you refuse to identify him, what else can I think?'

'Think what you like—Your Highness.' She managed to make the title sound less than respectful.

His next question caught her by surprise. 'How old are you?'

'Twenty-one, if it matters,' she said, startled and momentarily confused.

His hand went to her chin, tilting it upwards. She was distracted by the warmth in the wiry fingers. 'You look older. Your make-up, perhaps?'

Before she knew what was happening he'd whipped out a dazzling white handkerchief, monogrammed, she saw as he brought it to her face, and scrubbed the dark lipstick from her mouth.

The raw contact ignited a strange sensation inside her, half fury, half pleasure. She twisted her mouth away. 'Stop it. You may be a prince but you're no better than...'

His eyes gleamed as she swallowed the name just in time. 'So close to a confession. Perhaps there's another way to wring it from you.' He bent his head, bringing his mouth hard against her lips, which still tingled from his ministrations.

It was nothing compared to the liquid fire that seared her at his touch. The world slowed, heightening every sensation until she could have written essays about the heaviness of his hands on her shoulders, the warmth flooding her skin or the way his mouth moulded hers, giving and taking without quarter until she felt dizzy with a longing she'd never known before.

The ginger-scented air had serious competition from the musky fragrance of the prince's aftershave lotion, mingling with an air of masculinity, which was an aphrodisiac in itself.

All this happened frame by frame, like stop-motion, allowing her to absorb every singular sensation. The world didn't resume its normal speed until he stepped away from her, his expression severe. 'It's a confession of sorts, I suppose.'

She knew what he meant, and anger shrilled through her, both at her implied wantonness and at her uninhibited response to him. 'I suppose it's a treasonable offence on Sapphan to tell the prince to go to hell?'

His laughter mocked her. 'So the sex kitten is a tiger with claws? Pity you didn't unsheath them earlier to drive your unwanted suitor away.'

'I did,' she snapped wearily. 'For all the good it did me. Now may I return to my hotel, Your Highness?'

'Philippe will do,' he said silkily, 'since we've become so well acquainted.' He shrugged out of his immaculate white tuxedo jacket and draped it around her shoulders.

She was immediately enveloped in the scent of him, which clung to the expensive fabric. It was an effort not to inhale deeply, and she told herself it was the shock of the attack clouding her judgment. She started towards the palace. His hand on her arm stayed her. 'Where do you think you're going?'

Hadn't he amused himself enough at her expense for one evening? She'd more than paid for whatever sins he believed she'd committed. 'One of the crew will drive me back,' she explained.

'Not in that condition.' He snapped his fingers and a huge, dark-complexioned man materialised out of the night. Embarrassment flooded her skin with colour. She might have known the prince wouldn't be out here unguarded. 'Don't worry, Alec is all three wise monkeys rolled into one,' Philippe said. 'He will drive you back in my car.'

All the same she felt impossibly shy in the body-guard's presence. Only the thought that he must have seen his master kissing lots of women stiffened her resolve enough to hold her head high when he returned her to the hotel.

The reception had marked the end of the catalogue shoot. Instead of going sightseeing as planned with the rest of the crew, she rebooked her return flight to Australia for later the next day. It gave her time to have the prince's jacket dry-cleaned and returned to him at the palace. Her thank-you note was coolly reserved. There was no way she wanted him to know how badly his kiss had shaken her.

On the flight home she told herself she didn't care if she never went back to Sapphan. Her memories were of relentlessly hard work in steamy tropical heat, the unwelcome attentions of Alain Montri and a kiss from a prince who thought she was an amoral temptress.

CHAPTER TWO

THAT the kiss loomed largest in her memories there was no doubt, but Norah told herself it was because she disliked it so much. A prince Philippe might be, but he was also arrogant, overbearing and—and... She ran out of ands. She just didn't want to think about him ever again.

The last place she had expected to find herself was in his domain, at the fabled Pearl Palace in the capital city of Andaman. Not that they were likely to meet, given the heavy schedule Leon had told her Philippe was committed to. Even without that, the palace was big enough to keep her well away from him. More like a city than a home, it sprawled in a maze of over three hundred rooms divided into several pavilions. They were linked by tiered gardens, lush tropical greenery, pools and waterfalls. There was even a small zoo.

Norah was staying in the Jade Pavilion, beyond which was the Princess Pavilion, where Talay resided when she wasn't away at school, then the Watergate Pavilion, which contained the prince's apartments and innumerable wings for guests and servants. The grand ballroom alone would have housed several families.

Yet it wasn't a case of a wealthy monarch living in luxury while his people struggled. Talay had proudly informed Norah that the Sapphanese people enjoyed one of the highest living standards in the region, thanks to tourism and a bountiful pearl harvest, which gave the pearl kingdom its name.

Norah's gaze went to Talay, who drowsed in the late afternoon sunshine. 'I'll miss you when you're back at school tomorrow, Tal.'

Talay grimaced. 'I wish I didn't have to go. If I become a model like you, I won't need to study, will I?'

'Models need brains as well as looks,' Norah reproved gently, but was unwillingly reminded of Philippe's disdain for the modelling profession. It wasn't the reason she had given up modelling, she told herself, but she had to admit it had been an influence. Soon after returning to Australia she had enrolled at college to earn a degree in beauty therapy, using her modelling experience as a springboard. That her new career had also led to a disastrous love affair she hated to think about, and she forcibly dismissed it from her mind. Colin Wells was in her past, just like Philippe Rasada.

Talay nodded reluctantly. 'I suppose you're right. Maybe I will study, after all. Think of me slaving away trying to catch up on everything while you enjoy the last of your visit.'

'I will. Now you'd better finish your packing if you're to be in time for dinner with your friend's family. Scoot.'

With a last, heartfelt hug and a vow to see Norah before she went, Talay left. Restively, Norah looked around, finally deciding to visit the palace art gallery Talay had recommended. It was said to house nearly three thousand treasures from local and European artists in collections dating back several centuries.

Locating the gallery was easier said than done. Despite Talay's instructions, Norah was soon hopelessly lost among the winding walkways and courtyards, not recognising anything until she found herself in a walled garden presided over by Pompeian terracotta figures.

As she saw where she was, a shiver took her. This was the garden where Alain Montri had forced himself upon her.

A rustling sound made her spin around, and a dizzying sense of deja vu threatened to overwhelm her. At the entrance to the garden stood Philippe Rasada.

The evening sun painted the hard planes of his face in strong relief, emphasising the obsidian gaze fixed on her. Had he always been so tall, so massively built? Memories came flooding back, and she knew her mind hadn't exaggerated the power of his presence. Already it was reducing her to quivering silence as he inspected her as minutely as a slave on an auction block.

By force of will she subdued the tremors sweeping through her and made herself return the favour, noting the cleft that sculpted his strong chin and the lines radiating from either side of those compelling eyes. Humour or strain, she couldn't decide. He looked like a man who was very much in command of himself, yet shadows lurked there, too.

Realising what she was doing, she made an effort to collect herself. He probably didn't even remember her. 'Good evening, Your Highness,' she managed in a voice that was much less steady than she'd hoped. 'I apologise if I'm intruding, but I got a little lost.'

'Not for the first time, Miss Kelsey,' he said in the resonant, faintly accented voice she remembered so vividly.

Her heart sank. So he did remember her. It dawned on her that he was much less surprised by her presence than she was by his, almost as if... She dismissed the thought. 'I'll go now if you'll excuse me.'

He stepped across the narrow path. 'You weren't in such a hurry to leave last time we met here.'

Before she could restrain it, her hand went to her mouth, unconsciously tracing the line of his kiss. In horrified recognition, she dropped the hand. 'Please, Leon will be wondering where I am.'

'Leon will be delighted you're with me. It is his plan, after all.'

Confused, she shook her head. 'Leon's only plan was for me to help Talay deal with the scars left by her injury. I don't understand what you mean.'

'But you do know that Talay isn't the only reason for your presence here?'

Indignation drew her up. 'Of course, she is. You, of all people, must know I wouldn't come back for any other reason.'

His eyes slid over her, his expression a stone mask to equal the sculptures around them. 'No? Then you are a liar, Miss Kelsey.'

'You called me a liar before, Your Highness,' she snapped. 'It wasn't deserved then and it isn't now.'

He frowned. 'The first time remains to be seen, but this time it is certainly deserved. You returned because my kiss is burned on your memory as surely as yours is branded on mine.'

He couldn't know how many times she had relived it in the last five years, could he? Was it the reason she had allowed Leon to persuade her to return? Then her eyes went wide. Branded on mine, he'd said. Could the impact possibly have been mutual? No, she wouldn't allow that he was right. 'I hated what happened,' she said in denial. 'I would never have returned if I'd known we had to meet again.'

'Then why did you allow Leon to install you in the bridal pavilion?'

'But he didn't. Oh, no, the Jade Pavilion isn't . . . It can't be. . . .'

Her voice tailed away as something clicked into place. She had thought her suite luxurious, even fanciful, with its Chippendale furniture, a rug Talay said was made for Napoleon and Josephine and a carved four-poster bed inlaid with cream and gilt. Her face betrayed her anguished realisation. 'It can't be.'

'I see the truth is starting to dawn,' he mocked. 'Were you really so blind that you couldn't see Leon's plans for you? To him falls the duty of finding me a wife before my coronation.'

Leon had been so gently insistent on bringing her to Sapphan, despite her belief that she had done all she could for Talay in Australia. Now she saw why, and her breath escaped in a sigh of despair. 'Oh, no.'

'Oh, yes. You, my dear Australian minx, are Leon's choice of bride for me.'

The cold irony in his voice struck her like a blow. She drew herself up. 'Now just a minute. Surely I have some say in this?'

He made a dismissive gesture. 'Of course. You may choose your gown, your guests and attendants.'

'You know I don't mean the ... the trappings,' she said, incensed by his arrogant acceptance of the situation. 'I prefer to choose my own husband, thank you.'

Even thinking of the prince in such a way was enough to send her heart into a frenzied hammering, which she told herself was due to the craziness of the proposal. He was the last man on earth she would consider marrying.

He regarded her searchingly. 'How could there be any other choice of husband for you beyond the absolute ruler of a nation?'

The ruler of her heart, for one. 'I prefer to marry a man, not a position,' she stated. 'Where I come from, we do things differently.'

His expression twisted into a sardonic mask. 'I well recall how you do things—with no decorum, no sense of decency and no moral strictures whatsoever.'

She felt her face flame. 'You're judging me on very little evidence, Your Highness.'

'It was Philippe last time, and I make my judgments on the evidence of my eyes and senses.'

Something snapped inside her. 'You have no right to judge me at all.'

His dark eyes flashed at the implied challenge. 'On Sapphan I have all right. Our ancient laws grant me ownership of everything—and everyone—in the kingdom.'

Panic coiled through her, although she held herself outwardly rigid. 'Ownership of people is barbaric.'

'I didn't say I subscribe to it, only that the right exists.'

'To be held over the heads of your people like some sword of Damocles? Some democracy.'

Her taunt slid off him, leaving no trace. 'Make no mistake, Sapphan may be enlightened but it is not a democracy. My people rejected that style of government not once but several times. To them freedom cannot be legislated. It is a state of being granted to all as a birthright. They see no reason to write it into law when the proper concerns of government are economics and the wellbeing of the people.'

A shudder shook her. 'You see, your ways are alien to me. Leon can't seriously mean you to consider me as your consort?'

'He can and he does. And I respect his choice in the matter as I respect Leon himself.'

Feeling like Alice as she began her tumble down the rabbit hole, Norah shook her head. 'What about my choice?'

'You exercised it when you agreed to come and took up residence in the bridal pavilion.' He took a step closer, and her internal temperature soared. 'Is it such a terrible prospect, being chosen as a bride for a prince?'

A bride for a prince? Surely she was dreaming? Any moment now she would wake up in her own bed in Sydney, smiling indulgently at the fantasies a tired brain could conjure up.

But the fantasy persisted in the form of Philippe, large as life, and yes, she admitted reluctantly, twice as handsome. She could loathe his blue-blooded arrogance, but no feat of imagination could make him less than devastatingly attractive.

As a fan of old movies, she didn't need much prompting to picture him as Errol Flynn, down to the raffish strands of hair straying across his wide forehead. The cleft chin was hero material, too, except that Philippe was real. So was his outrageous proposal.

She shook her head. 'You can't hold me to a bargain I had no idea I was making.'

'And if you had known?'

'I would have run as far in the opposite direction as I could.'

The prince's level gaze held an expression she couldn't begin to decipher. 'Sapphan is an island kingdom. There isn't very far to run.'

Would anywhere be far enough from the extraordinary power of this man? The thought caught her by surprise. Part of her unwillingly recognised that it was this very power that had drawn her back to Sapphan against all logic and common sense. She forced herself to focus on what he expected of her.

'I . . . you can't be serious about me as a potential consort?' She had to force the words out.

He studied her narrowly. 'When will you accept that I can do anything I wish? My power here is virtually unlimited.'

Her throat felt stripped, raw. 'But not over me.'

'Are you quite certain?'

No, she wasn't, but she was damned if she was going to let him see it. His subjects might kowtow to him at every turn, but he was going to find out that he had bitten off more than he could chew with Norah Kelsey. She was going to treat him like any other man making an unwelcome proposition. She was going to...

She was going to drown in a sea of sensation as he took her in his arms and kissed her.

Struggle, resist, put some of your self-defence classes to good use, her brain ordered. Somehow the message got scrambled on the way to her limbs, which instead twined themselves around him, forcing their bodies closer as his lips made ever more demanding forays over her mouth and throat.

The rush of blood through her veins was like a thundershower, carrying away every inhibition she possessed until her knees weakened and her heart beat a frantic tattoo, which threatened her consciousness.

The palm he cupped to the side of her face felt fiery, his fingers unyielding as he explored the soft contours of her mouth. She had a wild urge to fasten her teeth onto his fingertip as he skimmed her lower lip. Before she could act he clamped both hands to the sides of her head and kissed her again, hard, with a possessiveness that took her breath away.

'No power over you at all,' he murmured as he lifted his head, his eyes brightly challenging.

Her laboured breathing made denials useless. She fought for control, her mutinous glare sliding harmlessly over him. 'Any power you might have over me is purely physical,' she said when she could speak again. 'You can't stop me thinking what I like, and what I'm thinking now is probably high treason on Sapphan.'

'What you're thinking may be scandalous but never treasonous,' he said, divining her thoughts so precisely that she felt her colour heighten. 'Perhaps Leon is more perceptive than you give him credit for.'

'All the same, I won't be bartered by him—or you. It's practically the twenty-first century. Women must have rights even in Sapphan. Even Leon can't deliver me into the marital equivalent of slavery.'

He folded his arms impassively across his broad chest. 'Leon is the oldest member of the ruling family, and constitutionally considered wisest in these matters. It is his absolute right to nominate the king's bride.'

He was discussing this as if it was a fait accompli, which she would never accept, never. 'What about love?' she demanded.

He shrugged. 'Love grows where the ground is fertile.'

The last shreds of her control snapped. 'Oh, stop talking like something out of the *Arabian Nights*. I'm a modern Australian woman with all the vices and virtues of my era. It hardly makes me the Cinderella type.'

His expression hardened. 'Nor is this a fairytale. It is reality, and you will do well to accept it. Leon has made his choice. I will honour it, as I honour him, and so will you.'

He was deadly serious. There had to be something she could do. 'You mean you would marry me, when you clearly think so little of me, out of an antiquated sense of duty and honour?'

'Honour and duty are not considered antiquated ideas in Sapphan. They have kept my country free, stable and prosperous for seventeen centuries. Perhaps you can learn something of them.'

'With you as my teacher, I suppose?'

She gasped as his hand grazed the side of her face. 'I would be your teacher in many things, Norah.'

Her throat burned as she tried to swallow a huge lump, which impeded speech. 'Go to hell, Your Highness.'

He gave a hard, mirthless laugh. 'That's the second time you've wished me there. Aren't you afraid I could have you beaten for such outspokenness?'

Her eyes fastened on his in mute challenge. 'I'm not afraid of you.' But she was, mortally afraid. Not of physical threats, because she knew the Sapphanese weren't a violent race. It was more the threat to her survival as an individual. Even as he appraised her she could feel herself drowning in the dark pools of his gaze, losing her will to resist this bizarre match he was intent on forcing upon her. 'No, please,' she whispered.

The tension inside her grew unbearable as he held her with his eyes, stripping away the last of her defences until she felt he knew her as well as anyone alive. With a soft oath, he spun away to rest his palms flat against a sculpted figure of a soldier, his fingers reading its texture like braille.

He seemed to be summoning control from somewhere deep within. 'There are some things even I will not do,' he said in a curiously clipped voice. 'Rejecting Leon's choice of bride is one of them. However, there is what you would call an escape clause.'

The expected surge of relief was slow in coming. 'There is? What is it?'

'If you bear me no heir within a reasonable time, you may be released from the union as inadequate.'

CHAPTER THREE

'Inadequate?' Hysterical laughter bubbled in her throat. 'I'd be your cast-off, in other words.' The thought of how long it would take to reach that stage, and what was involved in establishing it, drove the air from her lungs. It conjured up far too vivid images of herself in Philippe's bed. 'Can't we just agree right now that I'm—' she almost choked on the word '—inadequate?'

His taut gaze returned to her, and his fingers tightened visibly around the stone figure. 'But I have no proof that you are, do I? Unless—' his eyes roved over her long limbs, coming to rest on her flushed face '—you wish me to put you to the test. It can easily be arranged, tonight, if you desire.'

His suggestion brought her head up, her eyes blazing, although the fire the suggestion ignited inside her came from quite a different stimulus than rage. 'No, thank you. I have all the proof I need of how much I'd hate it.'

He gave an impatient sigh. 'Must you keep driving me to prove you wrong in these matters?'

Recalling his last demonstration, she recoiled. 'You are the most arrogant, insufferable—'

'Careful,' he intervened before she could complete the taunt. 'Remember whom you address.'

'How can I forget?' she tossed at him. 'Who else but an all-powerful ruler of his country could press me into marriage against my will until he can cast me aside for being inadequate?'

He gave a mirthless chuckle. 'Now I understand. Your objection is not to the marriage, but to the possibility of being found wanting.'

'You as much as said so, yourself.'

One dark eyebrow canted upwards. 'And this troubles you?'

He read the answer in her disturbed expression. 'Yes, it does,' she replied.

He couldn't know it, but he had touched a nerve sensitised long ago by parents who set impossibly high standards for her and were disappointed when she failed to meet them. Not that anything was ever said. It was the air of head-shaking sadness and murmurs of, 'It's all right, dear, you did your best.'

How they would laugh if they knew she was being auditioned as consort to the ruler of Sapphan. Their favoured son, David, was the one expected to carry on the family tradition of excellence. Never in their wildest dreams had her parents considered that Norah might achieve greatness. A bride for a prince. Not our little Norah. Yes, it was considered briefly but it wasn't to be. 'It's all right, dear, you did your best.'

His touch on her arm drew her back to awareness. 'Norah, what is it?'

'I was thinking about my family. They already consider me a failure because I chose modelling and beauty therapy instead of medicine, like the rest of them. This will really set the seal on their opinion of me.'

'Why should their opinion matter?'

'It shouldn't. But when you've been told all your life that you're second-best . . .' She looked at him with brimming eyes, but refused to give in to tears. 'They made no secret that they really wanted another son.'

The prince tilted her chin up. 'Are they totally blind to beauty?'

She blinked hard. 'In our family, it's considered the consolation prize. Brains are what matters.'

'They are not mutually exclusive qualities.'

She managed a tight smile. 'As a doctor, I make a great model.'

He snapped his fingers angrily. 'Enough. You will not deprecate yourself so in my hearing.'

'I suppose it wouldn't do to let the people think their prince's choice of bride is a bimbo.'

He was really angry now, the rugged jawline tight with the force of controlling it. 'Enough, I said. Can you not see that I have provided you with the means to exceed your family's wildest expectations? If you are my consort, they would be forced to bow before you.'

It was a heady thought, and she indulged herself with a second of wild imaginings before shaking her head. The price was simply too high. 'I can't agree.'

'Then you leave me no choice but to reject you publicly, giving as my reasons your behaviour on your last visit to Sapphan. Even Leon would have to accept such a decision.'

'But that would mean...'

'Precisely. The scandal would be headline news from here to Australia.'

She was trapped, and his expression said he knew it. It was so unfair that she wanted to lash out at him. Instead she balled her fists at her sides. 'You may have won for now, but you know I'll do everything in my power to escape this farcical union.'

He moved closer. 'Then I shall have to see what I can do to make it more acceptable to you. As my consort your power will be second only to my own—and power can be an extraordinary aphrodisiac.'

The two choices loomed in front of her like the gates of heaven and hell. Scandal and disgrace, which would confirm her family's worst fears about her—or the world he would place at her feet. Was there any real choice? 'Very well, I agree,' she said in a low voice she hardly recognised as her own. She fought the urge to retract the promise as soon as she made it. Heaven and hell? More like two different levels of Hades.

But it was too late.

'I also agree to our union,' he said in a curiously formal voice, then held out his hand to her. 'Come. We will set the seal on our bargain.'

He led her to a space that was part hallway, part cloister. Double columns set on either side of sliding glass panels framed the vaulted space, which was furnished with a filigree table and chairs. On the table an ice bucket held a glistening bottle of vintage French champagne. Two Bavarian crystal glasses engraved with the Rasada family crest stood on a gold salver. She eyed the goblets suspiciously. 'You were very sure of me.'

He opened the bottle expertly with the tiniest popping sound and filled the glasses, handing one to her. 'Perhaps I was sure of my ability to persuade you.' He lifted his glass and touched it to hers. 'Long life and prosperity.'

'Prosperity and long life.' She echoed the traditional Sapphanese toast and sipped the sparkling liquid, which teased her throat. 'It's wonderful.'

'A foretaste of the life you will enjoy as my wife,' he predicted. 'Drink only a little. You will need a clear head for your first official duty this evening.'

'I couldn't, it's too soon,' she demurred, her panic rising as she began to fully realise what she had done.

His expression was implacable. 'You can and you will. Tonight we host a reception in Leon's honour, in recognition of his services to my council of advisors, which, by custom, is dissolved on my coronation. Leon will expect to see you at my side.'

She fell back on the time-honoured excuse. 'I have nothing suitable to wear to a state occasion.'

'A selection of designer gowns will be brought to your suite within the hour. Your attendant will see to your every need and bring you to me in time for the reception. Unless you do not intend to uphold your part of our bargain.'

The implication was clear. If she did not, the scandal would follow her from here to Australia. A vision of her parents' reaction decided her. 'I'll be there.' But not for long, she resolved privately. There had to be a way out of this, and she intended to find it.

The problem occupied her mind as she was prepared for the state reception. Luckily years of modelling experience stood her in good stead as attendants fussed with her hair, her make-up and her gown. It left her mind free to do what it had always done on assignments—worry away at a problem like a terrier after a bone.

Except that this bone was the biggest one of her life. Philippe Rasada actually believed she would marry him because dear Leon sanctioned it. Didn't either of them care how she felt? Granted, Philippe was an attractive, charismatic man. If she'd had the slightest doubts, he had kissed them away to devastating effect this afternoon. But marriage . . .

Amari—was that her maid's name?—spilled two incredibly beautiful gowns over the bed. 'The Dior or the Hervé Léger?' she asked, her voice musically soft. Norah was tempted to ask her opinion of

Philippe's proposal, but Amari would invariably side with her prince. Like Talay, the young maid had a bad case of hero-worship where Philippe was concerned. No wonder, if half the things he was supposed to have done for his people were true. But did everyone on this island have to think the sun rose and set around him?

'The Dior, I think,' she said dismissively. It was almost nunlike in black crepe with a shoulder-wide winged collar of white satin. Nunlike if you didn't count the uncomfortable amount of décolettage, she thought, biting her lip. But it was less provocative than the fiery red of the Léger, with its chiffon straps and sheer skirt below the hip. It wasn't hard to imagine Philippe's gleam of approval if she wore it. Which was reason enough to reject it.

She lifted her arms as Amari slid the Dior carefully over her head. It skimmed her slender form to perfection, the midnight fabric emphasising the brilliance of her hazel eyes. Amari had performed some alchemy with make-up so her eyes looked huge against the cream of her model-flawless skin. Maybe she'd show Norah how she did it sometime.

'Perfection,' Amari murmured, standing back.

'I couldn't agree more.'

With a soft cry, Amari dropped to a curtsey as Philippe materialised in the suite. Norah remained defiantly erect. A spark of challenge flashed in the prince's eyes, assuring her he had noticed. *Later for you,* the look promised.

A shudder ran through her, but she refused to look away. In spite of herself, her emotions went on full alert at the sight of his regal bearing beneath the black and white evening jacket, wing-collared shirt and Yves Saint Laurent grey silk tie. She was caught for a moment by a clawing sensation of longing so intense it made her grip a chair back to steady herself.

Catching sight of her sudden pallor, Philippe frowned. 'Do you feel all right, Norah?'

This was the man who wanted to hijack her into marriage. How could she feel anything but fury towards him? 'I'm fine,' she said through clenched teeth. 'It's been a while since I've eaten, that's all.'

An angry jerk of his head sent Amari scuttling away to return moments later with a salver of hors d'oeuvres. 'I won't have you fainting in front of my guests.'

She forced herself to eat something, aware all the time of his pervasive presence. Some of the light-headed sensation passed, and she was able to take his offered arm with an aplomb she was far from feeling. Couldn't he see this was useless? She simply wasn't princess material.

If Philippe was aware of her trepidation he gave no sign, but kept her arm tucked in his as they made their way along a vaulted walkway to the ballroom where his guests awaited.

At his entrance, an orchestra struck up the Sapphanese anthem. During it she risked a glance at Philippe from under lowered lashes and was stunned at the glow that seemed to emanate from him. Whatever she thought of him privately, he was born to rule. There wasn't a man in the room who could hold a candle to him.

Much more of this and she'd be proud to be at his side, she thought, annoyed with herself. It was an effort to marshal her confused thoughts as a receiving line was assembled in front of them. The cream of Sapphan society moved past them, and Philippe had a few murmured words for every person. His memory for names of children and personal circumstances seemed inexhaustible. Suddenly tension rippled through Norah, earning a searching look from Philippe. 'What is it?'

'Someone I...I know,' she managed to say. It was Alain Montri, whom she'd last encountered in the sculpture garden five years ago. The memory of that night was still burned into her mind. She wanted to turn and run as he approached, but some part of her refused to give him that satisfaction. She drew herself up, emulating Philippe's ramrod-straight bearing. 'Good evening, Alain.'

His green eyes were coldly assessing, but his mouth curved into a smile. 'Good evening, Miss Kelsey. May I introduce my sister, Kitma Montri.'

The woman was breathtaking. Tiny of stature, like many Sapphanese women, she looked impossibly fragile, with lustrous raven hair coiled high on her head and almond-shaped azure eyes that flickered over Norah, taking in every detail at a glance. Her smile was pleasant enough, but her words left Norah nonplussed. She spoke in rapid Sapphanese.

If it was intended as a slight, Philippe ruined the effect by leaning closer. 'Kitma wishes to make you welcome in the traditional way, don't you, my dear?'

The woman inclined her head submissively, but not before Norah caught a flash of anger in the sea-green eyes. 'Of course, Your Highness,' Kitma said in softly accented English, and moved on with her brother before Norah could reply.

'Bitch,' she murmured under her breath.

She saw his eyebrows climb. 'I didn't catch that.' But she felt sure he had. 'I will arrange for you to take lessons in our language as a priority,' he added. She could have sworn there was a glint of amusement in the obsidian gaze he turned on her.

The thought buoyed her sufficiently to enjoy the rest of the evening. It was a pleasure to see Leon again, although he had the grace to look chastened when she chided him for getting her into this.

'It is an old man's privilege to keep some things to himself,' he said mildly.

'We'll discuss it later,' she said sotto voce, as a sudden hope surged through her. If she could con-vince Leon that this was a mistake, he might withdraw his endorsement of her. As if he sensed her scheme, Leon made himself very scarce after that, making it impossible for her to have a serious talk with him.

When he finally did come close enough for conversation, the orchestra struck up a lively waltz, and Philippe held out his hand to her. Her despairing look went to Leon, who gave an almost imperceptible shake of his head.

'No-one can dance until we do,' Philippe informed her.

Moving with Philippe to the centre of the vast ballroom with all eyes upon them, she felt horribly conspicuous.

'Relax, we are alone, completely alone,' Philippe whispered as he took her in his arms.

His palm was warm against her back, and he held her close, so she was disturbingly aware of every sculpted contour of his body. He was an excellent dancer, and fortunately so was she, dancing being one of the movement skills models were expected to perfect. Still, she had never before felt such harmony with another dancer as she did in Philippe's arms.

She floated rather than stepped around the ballroom, dizzyingly aware that he was right. They were alone. The rest of the world spun out of existence as his touch wove a private world around her.

She had intended to hold herself stiffly, to make him aware of her continuing displeasure, but it was almost impossible when her body insisted on melting against him with sinuous ease.

She was dimly aware that other couples had joined them on the floor and wished she had the nerve to simply walk away. Instead she stayed, and the music wove a capricious spell around her emotions until it was hard to recall what she was supposed to be so angry about.

Only when the prince was approached by another man did she awake from her trancelike state. 'An urgent telephone call for you, sir,' Alain Montri said deferentially.

Philippe frowned. 'Would you partner Miss Kelsey until I return?' His taut smile favoured her. 'Affairs of state, I'm afraid. I won't be long.'

'But...' Before she could voice her objection, Alain had slipped into the prince's place, and Philippe was striding across the ballroom, couples parting like the Red Sea before him.

'You arranged this, didn't you?' she hissed at Alain, trying unsuccessfully to tug her hands free of his hateful grasp.

He shrugged. 'Affairs of state, as Philippe said. He was awaiting news of a United Nations decision that affects our balance of trade.' Then he gave a sinister smile. 'But I agree, it is... convenient.'

'For whom?' she snapped. 'You know I never want anything to do with you again.'

'Which is why I'm surprised to see you in Sapphan,' he responded imperturbably, 'and installed at the prince's side. Leon has no business nominating a foreigner as his choice of royal bride.'

There was no point asking how he knew. In the palace news obviously travelled fast. 'Then you'd better take it up with Leon,' she retorted. 'It wasn't my choice, either.'

He looked dubious. 'You mean this isn't your idea?'

Her furious glare raked him. 'Like all the men in this kingdom, Leon takes what he wants and asks afterwards.'

To her astonishment, Alain tossed his head back and laughed, earning curious looks from the other couples circling the floor. 'My faith, that's rich. A twentieth-century bartered bride.' He sobered suddenly. 'Look, I want to apologise for my behaviour on your last visit. I'd been drinking and... well, you know how it is.'

His winning smile left her cold. 'No, I don't. I only know I trusted you and you took unforgivable advantage of me. If Philippe hadn't come along when he did...'

'Nothing would have happened, I swear. I would have come to my senses in time.' His gaze narrowed. 'I take it Philippe doesn't know all the details.'

'He blames me for what happened,' she said stiffly, sure that Alain's belated apology was only prompted by the discovery that she was very likely to be his new queen.

But it seemed he had his own agenda. 'I suppose you already know that Philippe is head over heels in love?'

She stumbled slightly but was supported by Alain's hold on her. 'What?'

'He and my sister, Kitma, have been in love for years,' he informed her.

A roaring sound in her ears brought a wave of dizziness. 'If it's true, why doesn't he—'

'Don't you see? He can't marry her while you are Leon's choice,' he said urgently.

It was Leon's right to choose the ruler's bride, she remembered dully. 'And Leon won't change his mind.'

'He's an old man. His mind may not be what it was. He probably thinks it's the greatest devilment in the world to force you onto Philippe.'

The thought that her selection might be no more than the capriciousness of a senile old man was painful to consider. Was it possible? Then she shook her head. 'Leon's mind is still sharp. He probably thinks it's a great compliment.'

'But you don't agree.'

How could she tell him that she was torn between feeling trapped by a match not of her own making, and feeling a curious elation whenever Philippe came within her orbit? 'I wasn't exactly given a choice,' she murmured, lowering her head to hide the sudden rush of colour to her cheeks.

Alain's hand tightened on her shoulder. 'Then let me make amends for my previous indiscretions. Let me help you to escape and leave the way clear for Philippe and Kitma to enjoy their happiness.'

CHAPTER FOUR

THE offer was tempting. If anyone but Alain Montri had made it, she wouldn't hesitate. But he had betrayed her too badly.

She felt the resistance flare in her eyes and saw him set his shoulders in a shrug. 'Your choice. A lifetime is a lot to spend with a man who loves someone else.'

Over Alain's shoulder she glimpsed Philippe in conclave with Leon, two other men and Kitma Montri. Her heartbeat quickened, and she hated herself for asking, 'What is your sister to Philippe?'

'Officially, his special envoy to the United Nations. Unofficially—well, you have only to see them together.'

Her eyes went to the group. Philippe's hand rested lightly on Kitma's shoulder in a confidential gesture. It might have been brotherly, until Norah glimpsed the warmth in his gaze and the closeness of their heads. Could it possibly be true? What was Leon thinking of, to impose his will when he must know how things stood between the prince and Kitma?

Second best. The words slammed through her mind with sickening force. It was happening again. Leon was trying to impose her on a man who wanted another. Staying meant accepting a lifetime of knowing she was second best. More than the shock of having the union forced upon her, this was almost beyond bearing. 'I can't,' she said, trying to choke the words back and failing.

'You can't stay or you can't leave? Which is it?' Alain's imperious demand sliced through the turmoil in her mind.

'Why must I decide now? I still don't trust you, Alain.'

His mouth tightened into a grim line. 'You have little choice, my dear. I'm the only one who can help you get out of Sapphan. Meet me tomorrow at two at the Guardian Temple in the city. Bring only what you can carry and your passport.'

It was all so cloak and dagger. And it was still Alain Montri seeking her trust. 'I don't know. I need to think about it.'

His expression turned ugly. 'Don't think too long, my dear. Under Sapphanese law, the honeymoon comes before the wedding ceremony.'

A gasp swelled in her throat. 'You're joking, surely?'

'I do not joke. In Sapphan, a couple is considered legally married from the moment they formally accept each other's proposal.'

Through her mind rushed a memory of Philippe's formality as he said, 'And I agree to the union.' Was it as simple and as final as that?

She tried and failed to conceal her shock from Alain.

'I see you recall the moment you became legally his wife. A ceremony merely sets the seal on the union.' He gave a wolfish smile. 'We consider it foolish to hold a ceremony before finding out whether the couple suit each other in every way.'

Panic coiled through her. Distantly she heard the waltz ending and doubted whether her legs would carry her to the edge of the ballroom. 'I don't believe you,' she said, although she was afraid he had just sealed her fate. Even coming from Alain, the words had the ring of simple, terrifying truth. A wife? Was it possible?

The dance ended, and he raised her hand to his lips in salute, his eyes mocking. 'Suit yourself. You'll find out soon enough. Tomorrow at two—if it isn't too late by then. For now, I must return you to your *husband*.'

The words were harbingers of doom. Her heart sank as he escorted her to Philippe, still chatting to his aides. The prince gave a tired smile when he saw her. 'Forgive me for deserting you. Norah. The UN chooses its own times.'

'But it was good news, I trust, sir?' Alain queried, his tone sickeningly deferential.

'Fortunately, it was.' Philippe brightened, returning his attention to Norah. 'With business done, I am free to enjoy the evening.'

Norah felt Kitma's glittering gaze tighten on her as Philippe led her to a banquet table where Beluga caviar glistened on mountains of shaved ice. She had never tasted caviar and did not do so now, although she swallowed a few mouthfuls dutifully. Her thoughts were too busy with Alain's revelation. Already a wife? It was as well she had swallowed or she would have choked on the delicacy.

'You look pale,' Philippe observed, studying her intently. 'You had quite a conversation with Alain. I hope he said nothing that has upset you.'

She set the silver plate and spoon down carefully, aware that her hands trembled. She locked them together and faced Philippe. 'He told me nothing I didn't need to know, such as the form of marriage on Sapphan.'

Disapproval flickered across Philippe's aristocratic features, and his gaze narrowed. 'How helpful of him. What exactly did he say?'

She strove for lightness and suspected she failed. 'It was some nonsense about a couple being married from the moment they formally declare their intentions.'

'It is not nonsense. We consider a marriage concerns only the two people involved. The union may be formalised later according to religious or secular custom, but it is official from the moment of mutual agreement, rather than from the date of a ceremony.'

Her rigid stance telegraphed her shock. 'But that means—'

He raised his champagne goblet to her. 'It means that under our law, you became my wife by mutual consent this afternoon.'

'And you didn't see fit to *tell* me?' Aware of the interested looks she was drawing, she lowered her voice to a husky, emotion-charged whisper. 'How many more shocks must I endure at your hands?'

His warm gaze left her in no doubt. 'Only one, and I promise it will be more pleasure than shock.'

'No.' Her denial was a tortured whisper. 'Never that.' Especially when she knew his heart belonged to another woman. However attractive she found him—and there was no point in denying it to herself, she *did* find him so—she drew the line at being second best in some things. In this, above all. 'I'm a foreigner, not bound by your laws,' she tried valiantly.

'Catch twenty-two,' he said for her ears alone, reminding her of his Western education. Added to French and British ancestry, it made for an incredibly complex individual. 'You ceased to be a foreigner when you became my wife.'

Her fingers lifted to her temples. 'This is outrageous. You know I'll never accept it?'

He shook his head. 'Your body is already accepting what your mind insists it rejects. However,' he continued over her attempted interjection, 'since our traditions are new to you, I shall delay our wedding night for the moment, to give you time to adjust to your new status.'

Her eyes flashed furious rejection. The reason for his sudden tolerance wasn't lost on her. It was standing only metres away, at the other end of the banquet table.

Kitma Montri, the woman he loved.

It was hard to be grateful for his forbearance when Norah knew her feelings had little to do with it. 'You're all heart, Your Highness,' she hissed.

'Philippe, please. Titles are inappropriate between us now.'

She shrugged, not betraying the sinking sensation that she was lost. 'You may accept that we've gone through some sort of marriage, but I don't.'

He swept away her anger with a grim smile. 'Guard your tongue, Norah, before I change my mind about giving you time to adjust. You goad me to prove to you that I *am* your husband. Is it what you want?' His taut face muscles relaxed fractionally. 'Perhaps it *is* what you want. Isn't there a saying in your literature about protesting too much?'

'Is it possible to protest too much when your freedom and your life are at stake?'

He gestured at the lavishness surrounding them. A deferential circle granted them privacy, although they were the focus of all eyes and interest. 'You are still free, and you are very much alive. Of that you will have no doubt when I do come to you, I promise.'

Her throat dried and she resisted swallowing, hating him to see his effect on her. The sudden, vivid image he conjured up was almost too much, especially when the real object of his affection stood nearby, her eyes flashing flame at Norah.

If looks could kill . . .

She lifted her head, meeting his gaze with all the defiance in her soul. 'And what about Kitma?'

There was an almost imperceptible tightening in his jaw. 'She is not under discussion here.'

Fighting a feeling of nausea, she heard the unspoken truth behind his words. It had to be faced. Might as well be now. Second best. She had not expected it to distress her so cruelly with someone she hated as much as she did Philippe Rasada. 'So it's true,' she managed huskily, 'you do love her.'

'Would it trouble you if I did?'

Not quite a denial, she noticed, and was surprised to feel shock and something else. Disappointment? 'Of course not,' she countered, wondering if he saw through her. He would think she cared when it was the last thing she felt. Any grief it caused her was purely at being second best again. How she hated the thought. 'Whom you love hardly matters to me, does it?'

'It matters to my wife, or it should.'

'*If* I was your wife. I still don't accept a bond made under duress—or in ignorance,' she added quickly when he moved to correct her.

'Your Australian legal system does not accept ignorance of the law as an excuse,' he reminded her, then gestured imperiously. 'We will discuss it no longer. The decision stands.' He followed her gaze to where Kitma watched them with blazing eyes. 'All other women are in my past. You are my future,' he said with a control bordering on savagery. 'It is decided.'

'But it's insane. If not for Leon, you wouldn't consider marrying me.' *Nor I you,* she wanted to add, but lacked the courage—for it couldn't be the conviction—to say it aloud.

He fixed her with a soul-deep glare. 'You are certain of that, aren't you?'

Of course she was. He didn't love her, didn't respect her. Only respect for Leon's prerogative prompted Philippe to accept her in place of Kitma. 'I have to be. It's the truth,' she said simply.

His dark eyes were unreadable, concealing the pain of being separated from his real love, she assumed. He hid it better than Norah knew she could have done. 'There are many truths,' he observed, lifting an eyebrow. He reached for her arm, frowning when she flinched. 'Come, it is time we danced again to allay rumours of our first lover's quarrel.'

For that, they would have to be lovers. Barely in time, Norah imprisoned the comment in her throat. He had accused her of goading him into making her his wife sooner rather than later. He hardly needed more provocation.

Dutifully she danced with Philippe and other nobles, made conversation and even managed to eat some of the magnificent supper provided. It was almost dawn by the time Philippe returned her to the Jade Pavilion. Exhaustion made her lean heavily on his supporting arm, her eyes almost closing.

'This day has almost been too much for you,' he observed, handing her into the suite. 'Shall I stay and tuck you into bed?'

Her eyes flew open, alertness rushing back. 'It's the last thing I need,' she snapped, picturing the scene with embarrassing clarity.

Judging by the dangerous glint in his eyes, he shared the vision. 'Still challenging me, Norah? When will you learn?'

She met his gaze defiantly, although her knees felt like buckling. 'When hell freezes over.'

With stunning swiftness, he tilted her face up even as his own head came down. The cry she opened her mouth to utter was silenced by the force of his mouth fastening on hers.

It was over almost before it began, but the effect of his kiss was electrifying, piercing her to her core with sensations she couldn't begin to assimilate, didn't want to, if the truth be known.

Her knees did buckle then, and he scooped her up with one strong arm around her shoulders, the other under her legs.

'What do you think you're doing?' she demanded, the tremor in her voice far too betraying.

She was very much afraid she knew, and hated herself for the shocking sense of anticipation that tore through her like the forerunner of a volcanic explosion. She didn't, couldn't want him to take her to bed. She didn't want him to take her anywhere, except possibly the airport. Yet every nerve crackled to life the instant he swept her into his arms.

The curious sense of living in slow motion returned. He held her as easily as a child, cradled against his chest as if she weighed nothing at all. It was a disturbing feeling, to be made to feel so slight, so boneless, when he was all bone and muscle and sinew against her.

Her head rested against his shoulder, and she felt his lips move over her brow. The palms that had been telegraphing her resistance against his chest slid up almost of their own accord to link around the strong column of his neck.

Then she was placed gently on the four-poster bed and he straightened. For a moment his face was unreadable, but she sensed he was fighting an internal battle. He reached down to kiss her swiftly again, in the manner of a parent bidding a child good-night. It should have reassured her. Instead she was assailed by a heart-wrenching sense of loss when he turned away.

'Philippe...' she began, then realised how close she was to asking him to stay. *Pleading* might actually be more accurate. She clamped her jaws shut on the words, her eyes flashing fire at him although it was much too little, too late.

His smile said he knew it. 'Don't look now,' he said with infuriating ease, 'but it just got distinctly chilly in Hell.'

Then he was gone, the door whispering shut behind him. With a belated rush of fury, she ripped off her dancing shoe and hurled it at the closed door. The soft leather slid to the floor harmlessly, but she thought she heard a throaty laugh from beyond it. Getting chilly in Hell, indeed.

Shocked at how near she'd come to proving him right, she jumped to her feet, certain of what she must do. She ran to the next room, stopping short as she encountered Amari, curled on a sofa, reading. At Norah's precipitate entrance, Amari looked up, startled. 'Is anything wrong, miss?'

Norah schooled herself to calmness. 'I'm surprised you're still awake, Amari.'

The girl looked shocked. 'Of course. You might need me.'

This was going to take some getting used to, Norah thought, then recalled her mission. Maybe she wouldn't have to get used to it, after all. 'I won't need your help preparing for bed,' she said evenly, 'but you can do an errand for me in the morning.' It was morning, she recalled distantly. 'Later, I mean.'

'What do you want me to do?'

Norah went to an antique escritoire under a bay window. A drawer yielded notepaper bearing the royal crest. Taking a sheet, she wrote rapidly, then placed the note in an envelope, sealed it and wrote a name on the outside. 'Will you see that this is delivered before breakfast?'

Glancing at the name on the envelope, Amari looked anxious. 'But this is to Alain Montri.'

The young girl must be shy of approaching someone of Alain's stature in the royal household. Norah smiled reassuringly. 'It's all right, he's a friend of mine. Will you see he gets the note? It's important.'

Still looking uncomfortable, Amari nodded. 'I will see it is delivered properly.'

Not surprisingly, Norah slept late, awakening with barely enough time to eat some of the breakfast Amari brought to her suite before she was due to say farewell to Talay.

'I am so pleased about you and Uncle Philippe,' Talay said with a shy smile.

Shock rippled through Norah. 'You mean you knew?'

'Not until last night, when Grandfather told me. It must have been a surprise to you, too.'

You don't know the half of it, Norah thought with a surge of frustration. Somewhere she found a smile. 'I'll miss you, Tal.'

The teenager's hand went to her face, her skin deceptively smooth under the concealing make-up. 'And I you. But we'll meet when I'm home from school, won't we?'

Knowing she would be long gone by then filled Norah with remorse until she thought of the alternative. She stroked the child's undamaged cheek. 'We'll always be friends, Tal.'

It wasn't an answer, but Talay accepted it, hugging Norah swiftly before following Leon's chauffeur to the limousine that would return her to boarding school. Tears pricked Norah's eyes as she spun away. If her plan worked, it would be a long time before she saw Talay again.

The hours passed slowly with Norah barely picking at morning tea, served in solitary splendour on a vine-clad terrace opening off her suite. At one o'clock she told Amari that she was going out. 'I believe the Guardian Temple is worth seeing.'

Amari concealed her disapproval well. 'Alec will accompany you.'

The behemoth bodyguard who had watched silently as Philippe kissed her five years ago. 'Don't bother Alec, I'll be fine alone,' she assured Amari, feeling a surge of remembered embarrassment. Alec was the last companion she wanted today.

But he was waiting when she reached the courtyard where the cars were kept. One glance told her there was to be no discussion. Either she went with him or she didn't go at all.

The Guardian Temple was the oldest on Sapphan, dating back to the thirteenth century in some parts. Even the supposedly new parts were two centuries old.

Norah tried to take an interest in Alec's tour-guide descriptions of what she was seeing as they drove slowly around the perimeter, but her heart raced so fast she felt close to collapse. In her shoulder bag were a few personal items and her passport, as instructed by Alain. She hoped Alec wouldn't insist on carrying it for her.

Royal status had its advantages, she discovered when they left the car at the entrance to the temple, in a space clearly off-limits to most cars. She was aware of Alec scanning the crowd around them with professional dispatch as he escorted her into the temple compound.

As she scanned the crowd for Alain Montri, Alec's summations barely registered. The temple contained the oldest metal images in Sapphan. There was also no back door, which meant that the temple wouldn't admit malevolent spirits. Weapons could be blessed here and their owners made invulnerable to knives and bullets.

The temple housed the longest religious manuscript in Sapphan, said to contain maps of buried treasure, Alec continued. Her surprised glance flickered to him. How did a muscle man know so much? And how on earth was she to escape his hovering presence?

A solution occurred when they reached a mural-clad pavilion guarded by carved statues of women. She didn't need the captions in English to realise this building was for women only. 'I'll only be a moment,' she said, smiling at Alec. She ducked inside before he could react.

She watched from the entrance long enough to see him step away, his back to the building, before she slipped behind the statues and into the shadow of the next pavilion.

It was the main hall of the temple, dedicated to the Goddess of Mercy. An omen, she hoped.

On the floor in front of the image were two containers of what looked like shaved chopsticks. As she watched, devotees picked up the containers and shook them rhythmically until one of the sticks worked its way to the top and fell to the floor. This stick was taken into an anteroom on the left. She tore her eyes away from the activity and searched for Alain. It was almost two, and the main hall was the most likely place to meet him.

'Not going to chance your fortune?' murmured a resonant voice close behind her.

Her heart slammed against her rib cage. Alain? Not even for an instant could she mistake the dark-suited figure leaning indolently against an alcove for Alain Montri. Even without Philippe's advantages of height and build she would have known him by that indefinable presence he radiated. Or was it just some damnable awareness of him she alone picked up?

She sagged against cold stone. 'What are you doing here?'

'Watching you.'

Her anger flared. 'Spying, you mean.'

'As you wish. Your note was specific as to time and place.'

She felt colour slash her cheeks. 'You read a private note?'

'Amari properly delivered it to me. Had it been harmless, I would have passed it to Alain. Under the circumstances, it was better not to involve an innocent man in your scheme.'

I shall see it is properly delivered. Oh, Amari, why didn't you simply take it to Alain? Philippe's cold gaze reflected the despair in hers as he lifted the bag from her nerveless fingers. Her heart sank as he retrieved her passport and slid it inside his jacket.

Accepting the bag, she felt something snap inside her. She was getting into the habit of thinking of herself as helpless. Well, to hell with that. There must be something she could do, if not now, then soon.

Philippe watched her face as if it was a television screen. 'Don't even think about it, Norah.'

His face was close to hers, his breath a disturbing zephyr against her cheek. She set her mind against the torrent of sensations his closeness threatened to unleash. 'There must be a law against kidnapping even on Sapphan.'

Laughter snapped in the cold black eyes. 'I am the law on Sapphan, a fact you may as well accept here and now.'

Never, her eyes said mutinously. What would he do if she planted herself here and simply refused to budge?

'I could have Alec carry you back to the car,' he said mildly, divining her thoughts with astonishing ease. 'Your choice.'

'Nice to know I have some left,' she snapped, but moved her feet. Being carried bodily to the car by Philippe's muscle man was an indignity she intended to avoid.

To her surprise, Philippe led her to the statue and handed her the can of fortune-telling sticks. She debated whether to throw them down then decided, why not? Maybe they would offer some shred of hope or a way out of her predicament. Nothing else seemed to be working in her favour.

She shook the sticks back and forth as the others did until one tumbled to the stone floor. Philippe read the number on it and steered her to the anteroom, where pigeonholes held slips of paper with corresponding numbers. He quickly located hers.

'The heart has answers; the mind only questions. Acceptance will bring you serenity,' he read with the faintest gleam in his eyes.

Her astonished look raked him. 'You're making it up.'

Gravely he handed her the slip. 'Have Amari translate it for you when we return to the palace.'

Somehow she knew what Amari would say. But they were both wrong. She would never accept her situation. Serenity was a long way off still.

Taking her elbow, he steered her out of the temple, leaving a donation as they left. Recognising the prince, the other visitors parted deferentially for them. It was a measure of the peaceful nature of their society that he could move around so freely, she couldn't help thinking. In most Western countries, he would have been surrounded by a phalanx of security people.

Alec didn't seem surprised when they emerged. Was she the only one not expecting Philippe to meet her here? 'I dismissed my car. Alec will return us to the palace,' he commented, although she hadn't asked. 'Unless you'd rather see more of the capital?'

'I wouldn't dream of imposing,' she said a little acidly, disappointment hanging heavily over her. She hadn't realised how much she'd counted on Alain's help. 'You may as well return me to my cage.'

His jaw tightened. 'One of the advantages of my position is the freedom to command my own time,' he said. 'Where would you like to go?'

'Home, to Australia.'

'Within reason,' he countered smoothly.

'Anywhere you like, then, since my choice is unacceptable,' was her angry response.

A strange glitter lit his gaze. 'I have the feeling that my first choice would be equally unacceptable.'

Her throat closed but she refused to swallow. Did it always come down to this with him? He was the most sensual man she had ever met. He stirred her blood in a way no-one had ever done before. It bothered her to see how easily he could fire her imagination with a veiled suggestion. He hadn't even needed to spell out where he wanted to take her before every nerve she possessed went on overdrive.

'Totally unacceptable,' she said in a strangled voice.

The wide shoulders moved in a shrug, which said, *Maybe for now*. 'Lunch, then,' he decided. 'It's time you tried some of our famous delicacies.'

As long as she wasn't on the menu, she thought, stirred by a sensation uncommonly like regret that he hadn't insisted on his first choice of destination. What was going on here? She hated the position he had forced her into. So why did lunch seem like such a disappointing option?

CHAPTER FIVE

THE air-conditioned limousine was a welcome relief after the heat and congestion of the temple compound. Norah was glad the roomy interior kept her apart from Philippe, although they may as well have been touching from the tumultuous way her senses insisted on reacting.

He looked coolly confident in a dark business suit and gleaming white shirt with maroon tie. Was there some genetic edge that kept royalty from perspiring? She felt horribly hot and uncomfortable even in the peach silk shirtwaister she'd worn in hopes of being on her way to Australia by now.

He handed her a glass of iced water from a refrigerator built into the passenger compartment. 'Drink this. It will cool you down.'

She took the glass and drank but couldn't resist saying, 'I suppose I'll be offered bread next. It *is* the accepted diet for a prisoner, isn't it?'

He looked grim. 'I agree that after today's performance, confinement would be appropriate. However, I have a much more suitable alternative in mind. Tomorrow I leave for the royal estates at Chalong where Leon and I will prepare for the festivities leading to my coronation. You will accompany me.'

Some demon of self-assertion drove her to ask, 'And if I refuse your invitation?'

The muscles tightened along his jaw. 'It is not an invitation.'

No, it wouldn't be. To cover her frustration, she looked around. She saw that they had arrived at a glassed-in restaurant on a hill overlooking the city, the port of Andaman and the azure waters beyond.

The royal standard fluttering on the car brought more fluttering from the restaurant manager and staff. In mere moments they were seated at the best table in a circular alcove with spectacular views at their feet and a screen of lush greenery between their table and the other diners.

'I hope you like seafood,' Philippe said. She had declined to study the menu, which meant little to her as it was written in Sapphanese script. With a shrug, Philippe ordered for her. As he raised his wineglass in a mocking toast, the corners of his full mouth lifted slightly. 'They were a little short of bread and water.'

She ignored her own glass, although her mouth was arid. 'Whatever is served I shall probably choke on it,' she vowed. 'I still can't believe you intercepted a private note addressed to someone else.'

The faint smile vanished. 'Believe it. Everything you do concerns me, Norah.'

'I know, I know—because I'm your wife.'

His feral look transfixed her. 'Are you finally acknowledging the fact?'

'In your dreams.' She did drink the wine then, but only to still the sudden hammering of her pulses. She wouldn't acknowledge it as fact for an instant. It simply slipped out. She would have to watch her tongue more carefully. It wouldn't do to give him ideas—well, more than he had already.

In spite of her promise, she enjoyed the food, which came as a welcome distraction from her churning thoughts. The first course was a spicy soup seasoned with lemon grass, filled with whole shrimps and prepared in a charcoal-heated tureen. It was followed by a seafood casserole in a coconut mousse made with chunks of fish and shellfish.

She refused the offer of coconut milk ice cream in favour of a simple platter of papaya, pineapple and watermelon peeled and cut into bite-sized chunks. The pineapple was tougher than she was used to, but deliciously sweet and refreshing.

A hot, very thin Chinese tea completed the meal. 'The Chinese prefer this on a hot day. They think ice is bad for the stomach,' Philippe informed her when the steaming brew was put before them.

'They're right,' she agreed. Beyond the first flush of heat from the tea, it was curiously cooling. She needed it after the spicy meal, she told herself. Her soaring body temperature had nothing to do with Philippe's closeness or the prospect of accompanying him to some outpost. 'Where is Chalong?' she asked.

'Only a couple of hours' drive away along the northwest coast,' he informed her. 'Our secondary airport is just south of Chalong. You may have flown in there from Australia.'

'No, we came to the main airport near the capital. Do you fly to Chalong?'

'Occasionally, when time is short. This time we'll travel by road so you can see something of Sapphan on the way.'

The prospect of a long drive with him unnerved her more than she allowed him to see. 'Is Leon travelling with us?'

Her faint hope was quickly dashed. 'He left for Chalong this morning in order to rest before we begin work.'

Concern for the dear old man overtook her anxiety. 'Rest? Leon isn't ill, is he?'

'He has not been well since the tragedy that killed his son and daughter-in-law and injured Talay. Accompanying her to Australia severely drained him.'

She didn't bother to hide her disapproval. 'Yet you let him undertake the journey?'

His icy look appraised her. 'One does not *let* Leon do anything. He is a man of strong convictions and even stronger will.'

It runs in the family, she thought grimly. She rested her chin on one hand. 'He never told me what happened. Was it some kind of tragic accident?'

His expression hardened. 'It was a terrorist bomb, planted on a runway they knew the royal party would be using.'

Coldness locked around her throat. 'Local terrorists?'

He shook his head. 'Outsiders, trying to sow discord among my people. They did not succeed. If anything, the attempt brought us closer. The people saw the attack on me as an attack on themselves.'

The icy fingers tightened their grip, almost strangling her shocked question. 'On you? You were aboard the plane, too?'

Almost without conscious awareness he touched a faint scar that marred his forehead just under his hairline. She had noticed it before but assumed it was the legacy of some sporting misadventure. She felt the colour leave her face and wondered why it should shock her so to think of him in mortal danger. Of course, she came from a medical family. It was simple human compassion.

'A commendable act,' he said, observing her reaction. 'You almost convince me you're pleased I escaped with my life. It would have simplified your existence if I had not.'

She did blanch then. 'Good grief, Philippe! You think I'd actually wish that on you, on anyone? How cold-hearted do you think I am?'

He looked thoughtful. 'From your work with Talay, I would have said not at all. This morning you gave me reason to reconsider my opinion.'

Feathery lashes dropped over suddenly moist eyes. It hurt to have him think so badly of her, but she was damned if she'd let him see it. 'I gave you fair warning that I wouldn't accept this situation.'

'But I did not expect you to involve an innocent man in your foolish attempt.'

Alain was anything but innocent, but there was no point in trying to explain. Philippe wouldn't believe her now any more than he would have done five years ago. What was it about blood being thicker than water? Alain was also of royal blood, and Philippe was in love with Alain's sister. How could she fight against a package like that?

She spread her hands palm upwards in a gesture of appeal. 'I have responsibilities, too, you know. You mentioned how I helped Talay. There are other teenagers like her at home depending on me. If I don't go back—'

'Your relief therapist will take over,' he cut in smoothly, earning a wide-eyed look. 'Yes, I had such details checked as soon as Leon told me of his choice.'

Her parents? Had they already heard about this?

He read the panicked question in her eyes. 'I've kept the news from the Australian media to give you time to inform your family.'

Her scowl washed off him, leaving no trace. 'How big of you, Your Highness. It never occurred to you that my parents would have appreciated being told *before* the wedding?'

'You misunderstand. Our marriage is official from the date of consent, but there is still a ceremony, which takes place as part of the coronation festivities. I shall arrange for your family and close friends to attend.'

Thinking of a wedding ceremony brought a new flush to her features. She was glad her family didn't yet know. Maybe they need not, if she could think of a way out of it. The trip to Chalong gave her an idea. Maybe she could still convince Leon that she was the wrong choice of bride for Philippe. Without Leon's endorsement the prince had no reason to keep her here.

She schooled her face to innocence. The last thing she wanted was for Philippe to suspect her plans and keep her away from Leon. Her hand tightened around the glass as she groped for a change of subject. 'You keep talking about your coronation. I thought you were already the absolute ruler.'

'Ruler, yes. Absolute, not yet. For the last nine years I have ruled as prince with the aid of an advisory council headed by Leon. By custom, the council is dissolved and I rule alone as king from my thirty-first birthday. I shall take a wife and a crown on the same occasion.'

She felt herself flushing. 'You make me sound like some sort of... accessory. A crown and a wife, like a matched set.'

'It can be seen another way. Just as the king takes the crown to rule over his kingdom, he also takes a wife to rule over him. It is a desirable balance, to avoid the corruption of too much power.'

He made it sound ideal. 'If the wife is willing,' she murmured. 'And don't give me that stuff about protesting too much.'

He regarded her coolly. 'Why should I, Norah? It is in your voice and your body language. Even as you protest, you sway towards me like a fern in the wind.'

Startled, she pulled back. Unawares, she *had* been leaning towards him. 'As absolute ruler, can you do anything you wish?'

He nodded. 'There are few constitutional limits on the power of the king.'

Her breath tightened in her chest. 'Then you could let me go.'

His dark eyebrows lifted dangerously. 'It is not so simple.'

'Why not? Just make a decree or something that from now on the king picks his own wife. You could have Kitma Montri and I could have...' She fell silent, aware of having talked herself into a trap of sorts.

He leaned closer. 'Who would you have, Norah? My investigations reveal no great love in your life.'

She might have expected him to check such matters. It wouldn't do to unearth a scandal after the wedding. 'There's no-one at the moment,' she said, hating the defensiveness that crept into her tone.

His long fingers tilted her chin up to him. 'Not since Colin Wells,' he observed, taking as confirmation the shock she was unable to entirely conceal.

She jerked her head aside, aware of a burning sensation where his fingers had gripped her. It was all she could do not to massage her chin, betraying his effect on her more than she wanted him to see. 'I'd rather not talk about Colin,' she said.

'But you don't object to discussing Kitma Montri. Come, Norah, turnabout is fair play, isn't that the Australian idiom?'

Sometimes she wished his education hadn't been quite so international. 'All right, we won't talk about Kitma,' she said. 'Is that fair enough?'

To her astonishment, there was a trace of concern in the dark gaze before he hooded it. 'Wells must have hurt you very badly.'

An echo of pain shot through her. Colin was a surgeon, a colleague of her brother's. David had introduced them. What he hadn't thought to mention was that Colin was married with two children.

Colin had made Norah feel like a queen until it came to a choice between her and his wife. 'If you must know, I was the one who left him,' she told Philippe defiantly.

'After you discovered he was married to a wealthy woman he had no intentions of divorcing,' he said.

Her angry gaze flashed to him. 'Did you expect me to do anything else?' Then she looked at the table. 'Of course, you did. Someone of my questionable morality wouldn't care if the man she loved belonged to someone else.' Choking, she was forced to stop.

Philippe took a breath. 'Loved, Norah?'

She forced herself to smile. 'Hardly, especially when I found out he was only using me to gain promotion at the hospital, hoping I would influence my brother on his behalf.'

Philippe's appraisal was long and thoughtful. Could it be compassion she saw in his eyes? It vanished before she could be sure. 'Why did you give up modelling and become a beauty therapist?' he asked unexpectedly.

He'd probably laugh if she told him it was because of him. Somehow he had made her feel as if she was wasting her talents and her life. Lord knew, her parents had believed so, without the talent part. Then a man she barely knew had rammed the realisation home with no more than a disdainful look and a few words.

With a finger she traced circles on the snowy linen tablecloth. 'Maybe there was more money in beauty therapy.'

He frowned. 'You were reputedly one of the highest-paid models in Australia. I wouldn't have had anything to do with the change, by any chance?'

She grimaced. 'You flatter yourself, although you did make your feelings about the value of modelling quite clear.'

He shook his head. 'My condemnation was of your behaviour. It wasn't a blanket judgment, and you did give me ample reason for it.'

'As you saw it.'

'There was no other way to see it. You flaunted yourself until one of my guests accepted your implied invitation, then you cried foul. I would have been more readily convinced of your innocence if you had been willing to name your so-called attacker.'

Throwing her table napkin down, she leapt to her feet. 'There you go again—my so-called attacker. How prejudiced can you get?'

She drew a sharp breath as his hand clamped around her wrist, the strength in his grasp unbelievable. It was either subside into her seat or risk a damaged wrist.

The obsidian eyes didn't waver. 'In Sapphan, there is a concept borrowed from our Thai neighbours called *chai yen*, a cool heart. It means that extremes of emotion, however justified, rarely produce the desired result. You would more readily change my opinion of you by example than by throwing useless temper tantrums.'

'You assume I want to change your opinion of me,' she snapped, massaging her wrist pointedly, although he had done no damage other than to her pride.

He remained unmoved. 'You still haven't answered my question. Why did you give up modelling?'

'My own choice.' *Nothing to do with your opinion,* she thought mutinously and wondered how true it was. 'I grew up in a medical family but I thought medicine wasn't for me. I finally found a niche where I could do some good.'

'Talay tells me you hope to open your own clinic in time.'

She nodded. 'It's a dream, to have a place where youngsters like Talay can regain their self-esteem after illness or accident.' She added unhappily, 'At least it *was* a dream, until I was lured here.'

'It needn't end here. With the resources I command, you could have your clinic in Sapphan, under royal patronage.'

Temptation rose like a living thing within her. The dream had been growing ever since she saw the results she could achieve. Then she sensed a trap. He was offering her the one inducement that might make her accept her gilded cage. 'No, I won't be bought,' she said fiercely.

He smiled thinly. 'Everyone has a price. Yours is at least commendable.'

'But still a price. I'm not for sale.'

'Everyone is hostage to some dream, even you. It's really only a matter of settling the details.'

Her legs tensed but she remained in her seat, her wrist tingling a reminder. 'If you think you can bribe me to accept this marriage—'

'Not bribe, compensate,' he cut in smoothly. 'I realise you are giving up a great deal—your home, your family.'

'My soul, freedom, honour,' she added.

'You are being unnecessarily melodramatic.'

'Am I? You said yourself I practically sold myself as a model. Flaunted myself, as you put it so graphically. Doesn't it make me ineligible as princess material?'

His jaw set. 'If I required perfection, princesses would be an endangered species. Fortunately, I do not require perfection.'

Coldness invaded her. 'What do you require, Philippe?'

His finger stroked the inside of her wrist, finding the pulse point, which had begun to hammer. 'You have not realised it yet? I want you.'

She could hardly summon her voice. 'Because I'm Leon's choice?'

He took his time answering. 'No, because you are my choice.'

Her blood was a thundershower through her body. It was the last thing she had expected him to say. 'Why?'

Shifting his grip to her chin, he turned her head gently but irresistibly until her eyes met her mirrored reflection on a far wall. His dark head was angled close to her fair one. In his grasp, she looked fragile and feminine. Her skin bloomed with colour and her hair tumbled in waves onto her shoulders. Modelling had enabled her to see herself objectively, as others did. All the same, it was hard to credit the glow she projected. No cover photo, with all the technical and cosmetic help in the world, had ever made her look so ethereal.

'I see you perceive the attraction,' he said dryly.

She turned confused eyes to him. 'Sapphan is full of beautiful women. Any one of them would gladly be the consort of the king.'

'Perhaps their very willingness disqualifies them.'

Her thoughts whirled. The lure of the unattainable? If it was the source of her attraction, what would happen after he attained her? Her heart sank as she followed the thought. He wanted her *because* she was unattainable. This was all an elaborate charade to fulfil his constitutional obligations while leaving his heart free to pledge to Kitma. Philippe wasn't capitulating to Leon's wishes. Leon was playing right into the prince's hands.

Nothing else made sense. He probably thought Norah deserved it after her supposed misbehaviour five years ago.

She felt as if all the breath had been driven from her body. He was using her, just as Colin had used her. And he had the nerve to question her morality? 'Can we leave now?' she asked in a low voice.

His hand covered hers, and it was all she could do not to snatch hers away. 'I see I have shocked you, my dear Norah. I'm delighted it is still possible.'

'You mean there's hope for me yet?' she retorted.

'There was always hope. Now that you understand your role here, it may become more palatable with time.'

Never in a thousand lifetimes, she vowed, then recalled the ideal of the cool heart. If she kept her feelings to herself, he might alow her the freedom she needed to change Leon's mind. Maybe there was merit in this *chai yen* idea after all.

If only it wasn't so hard to practise.

The limousine waited for them as they made their way through the restaurant, attended by the manager. Before they left, Philippe said a few words to the man and they were shown into a vast, spotless commercial kitchen. Instantly the staff scrambled to attention, but Philippe waved away the formality.

Norah watched in astonishment as he moved from one person to the next, exchanging a few words and earning beatific smiles in return. She couldn't understand the language but gathered that he was expressing his appreciation of the meal and service.

'It was kind of you to thank them personally,' she said when they returned to the car.

'And you don't associate me with kindness?' he second-guessed her.

'I haven't had much reason to so far.'

He took her hand and brought it to his lips, the touch bringing a fresh wave of colour to her cheeks. 'A situation I intend to rectify,' he assured her.

For appearances' sake, or to appease her so she wouldn't object to his continuing liaison with Kitma? Revulsion at either prospect overtook her, but not before her insides clenched at the very idea. His attention wasn't what she wanted, but some primitive part of her responded to him anyway. 'Stop it,' she hissed as much to herself as to him. 'I hate this, when I know so little about you.'

'Desire needs only the information of the senses,' he told her imperturbably. 'However, if it amuses you, Leon has an excellent collection of family photos and memorabilia at Chalong.' He regarded her keenly, her hand still imprisoned against his chest. 'I take it this sudden interest in my personal history does not indicate your surrender to the situation?'

'You never know,' she said lightly, awareness of him flashing along her imprisoned hand like a lightning bolt, to strike somewhere close to her heart. To her surprise, she was curious. What was he like as a child, a boy, a young man? To quell the sensation she added, 'It probably comes under the heading, know your enemy.'

He released her hand. 'Rest assured I shan't let your newfound interest go to my head. After this morning, I shall keep you under much more careful scrutiny.'

She almost welcomed the warning as safer ground. 'Why don't you lock me in the palace dungeon and be done with it?'

'In the first place, it would be a terrible waste. And in the second, the dungeons were converted to wine cellars a century ago. Besides, I'd rather have you where I can keep an eye on you. As I demonstrated in the restaurant, the surveillance promises to be quite pleasurable.'

For you, too, was the clear implication. Why didn't he stop this? Hating him was much simpler when he didn't insist on sending every nerve ending she possessed onto full alert. 'You can't watch me every minute,' she muttered.

He settled his shoulders. 'Good of you to forewarn me. Alec will drive us to Chalong. While I'm occupied with business affairs, he will be at your side.'

'He has to sleep sometimes,' she said recklessly, goaded beyond caring by his arrogance.

She regretted it almost instantly. 'Naturally,' he agreed. 'Therefore the nights will be my concern. From now on you will share my apartments, as befits your status.'

A chill ran through her, and something else she didn't care to examine. Surely not anticipation? 'No,' she denied emphatically. 'I will not share a bedroom with you. Some things even a king cannot command.'

He made a noise deep in his throat. It might have been a chuckle or a note of warning, or both. 'Some things a king doesn't *have* to command. I assure you, dear Norah, you will come to me willingly, and very soon. I think you protest so because you know in your soul that you want it to happen.'

A shudder gripped her. She couldn't allow that he was right. 'You've been reading too many fortune-telling sticks,' she denied, gazing sightlessly at the thronged streets leading to the palace.

'Possibly.' He slid a hand inside his jacket and took out a piece of paper she recognised from the Guardian Temple. She hadn't even seen him take a numbered stick. She snapped her lips together against the question she wanted to ask.

He answered it anyway. 'It says, ''There is much to be overcome, but your heart's desire will be attained.'''

She understood even better than he realised. She was the means by which he would overcome the obstacles to his heart's desire—union with Kitma Montri. She turned her face resolutely to the window so he wouldn't see the distress the realisation caused her.

CHAPTER SIX

TRAVELLING with a prince was a surreal experience. Norah had expected to get into the limousine with Philippe and simply drive to Chalong with Alec at the wheel. She hadn't anticipated a procession of several cars carrying staff, various aides and attendants, and more luggage than she needed when she moved house.

They rode in a Range Rover, which Philippe said would better cope with the steep hills on the road to Chalong Valley. The vehicle was spacious, but not as roomy as the limousine, so each time the car spun around a bend, their bodies touched. However fleeting the contact, she still reacted as if stung and grew increasingly irritated with herself for the reaction.

Philippe misunderstood her unease. 'Was it too early a start for you this morning?'

'We didn't leave until nearly nine. Back home I'm often at the hospital before eight.'

He held up his hands in mock surrender. 'Sometimes I forget that you aren't a hothouse flower.'

Like Kitma, she read between the lines. Reminding him of the difference seemed suddenly vital. 'As a model I was often out on location at dawn,' she stated flatly. 'The colder the morning,

81

the more likely I'd be wearing swimwear. I think photographers take courses in sadism before they're let loose to work with models.'

The set of his shoulders told her he disliked being reminded of her former career. Well, it wasn't as if she'd done anything illegal—or immoral, come to that. And he wanted to marry her. *What you see is what you get,* she thought mutinously.

She went on deliberately, 'One morning I had to pose in a tiny string bikini on the shore of Sydney Harbour on a freezing winter morning. I had to lie in a hollow in the sand while the photographer sprinkled frigid water over me so the droplets would sparkle in the morning light.'

Turning sideways, Philippe locked eyes with her. 'Enough. I know why you're reviving such memories.' His mouth tightened. 'I can even admit to admiration. You will not give in, even against me. But you will not speak of such things when we are with Leon. Is that understood?'

Her embroidering of the tale had been intended to taunt him, she acknowledged a little ashamedly. Not that he didn't deserve it. But Leon didn't, even though he had gotten her into this mess. His intentions were honourable. He probably thought he was doing her a favour. Chewing her lower lip, she managed a nod of agreement. 'I understand.'

His hands fastened on her upper arms, the grip light but irresistible. 'Then you will play your part while we are at Chalong?'

How far did he mean this to go? Her mouth was dry as she asked, 'My part?'

'As far as Leon is to know, you are delighted with the arrangement between us.'

She felt her eyes cloud. 'I have enough respect for Leon not to make any trouble, but delighted? I'm not sure I can go that far.'

His gaze remained locked with hers, the look filled with promise. 'Then it is up to me to induce delight by whatever means I can.'

'You...you wouldn't. I'd scream the place down.'

The disapproving shake of his head belied the sudden warmth that blazed in his eyes. 'You're certain you would want to? I don't recall much screaming the last time I kissed you.'

The memory made a tight knot of sensation inside her. She pushed it angrily away. 'It's difficult to scream when you have a mouthful of prince.'

He arched an eyebrow. 'Difficult to scream when every instinct is urging surrender,' he amended. His look softened so fleetingly that she wondered if she'd seen it at all. 'Did you think I wouldn't be able to tell?'

Her chin lifted. 'Did it ever occur to you that I might be acting? Faking my response?' It was suddenly vital that he believe it, because she wasn't sure she did.

His look said she'd been read like braille. 'Such a virtuoso performance,' he said, his voice dripping sarcasm. 'You should have no difficulty in convincing Leon of your—delight—in the arrangement.'

Caught as neatly as a fly in a spider's web, she realised hollowly. Either admit that her response to Philippe's kiss was not an act, or stick to her story and be required to continue the act for Leon. She was afraid she knew which was the lesser of the two evils. 'Then I'd better brush up my acting skills before we reach Chalong,' she answered.

His mirthless laugh taunted her. 'Don't work too hard. Leon is a much less discerning audience than I am, at least where you are concerned.'

She clamped her mouth shut, refusing to give him any more ammunition. His last taunt showed he had ample already. When would he use it? When he was ready, she concluded, and drew a shuddering breath to the limit of her lungs. He had as good as wrenched a confession out of her that she enjoyed his lovemaking. His look said he had no doubts. What about her own?

She submerged them in studying the passing landscape. Until now she'd been only peripherally aware of the road unwinding like a pale ribbon through jungle-covered hills and rubber plantations. Now she noticed the towering trees, ferns and exotic palms crowding the road. Here and there the brightness of a flame of the forest tree or the silvery glint of a dolphin palm caught her eye.

Despite the turmoil in her mind, she found herself enjoying the exotic scenery. Between stretches of dramatic limestone hills came rice paddies dotted with lolling water buffaloes, white egrets perched on their backs. Elsewhere rubber trees arched over the road like the buttresses of a cathedral, creating a church-like stillness as they passed beneath.

Chalong itself was on the other side of a pass, which Philippe informed her rose three hundred metres above sea level. At the top, she gasped at the beauty of the sea-fringed valley spread out below. Alec drove slowly, in low gear, and she understood the need for a four-wheel-drive vehicle. The grade was steep and dangerous. When Philippe's hand closed over hers she was nervous enough to appreciate the gesture of reassurance.

At the bottom she was trying to work out how to retrieve her hand when they drove across a concrete causeway and passed through a busy market town. From there the road followed the coast to a set of massive wrought-iron gates bearing the royal crest. The gates swung open as Philippe's car approached, and a sentry came to attention as they drove in.

The main building of the estate seemed to rise out of the jungle like an Inca palace, around which individual chalets looked like a village skirting the palace walls. Beyond them a wooden walkway sliced through the jungle and ended at a small, perfect private beach.

Every view could be framed as a watercolour, she thought. Intricately marked fireback pheasants strolled among stands of casuarina trees. There were bright pink rose apples, spiky red rambutans and a small grove of shiny-leaved cashew nut trees. It was a veritable Garden of Eden.

'Tonight you'll fall asleep to the sound of waves breaking along the shore,' Philippe murmured, watching her face.

She did pull her hand free then, closing down the interest sparkling behind her eyes. He must have brought her here hoping she would be enchanted enough to accept her situation. 'A gilded cage is still a cage,' she said.

He didn't blink. 'But better than the dungeons at the Pearl Palace.'

Remembering they were now the wine cellars, she made a face. 'At least I could have drunk myself into oblivion there.'

'Chalong has its share of intoxicants,' he countered. 'The sea, the jungle, even the fragrant air is said to be an aphrodisiac.'

She tossed her head in denial, although she was already aware of a dangerous lethargy creeping over her. 'Not that I'm likely to test it. This is supposed to be an act, remember?'

'There's no harm in striving for realism.'

As long as it didn't confuse the issue, she thought. She had promised to put on a good face, but she hadn't said anything about not talking Leon out of the whole idea. She would need to keep her wits about her if her plan was to succeed in such an earthly paradise.

Each pagoda-roofed chalet was a separate apartment with its own living room and bedrooms, butler's kitchen and staff quarters. The villa she was to share with Philippe was larger and grander than the others, with its own pool and waterfall in a clearing surrounded by rainforest.

Inside, the walls were lined with aromatic eagle-wood, the precious heartwood so rare it was once used as a form of currency. Gold glinted off taps and light fixtures, and the furniture was rattan and bamboo with hand-printed silk coverings.

The staff took over the unpacking immediately, leaving Norah with nothing to do after her first look around. She approached Philippe, who was already conferring with an aide. 'I think I'll call on Leon and pay my respects.'

He shook his head. 'Impossible. His doctor has confined him to bed for the moment.'

The blow to her plans was overtaken by concern for Leon, for whom she had a very genuine liking. 'Is it serious?'

He shook his head. 'He mainly requires rest, and I know from experience how difficult it is to persuade him to take things more easily. One would think the coronation depended exclusively on him.'

'Doesn't it?'

He looked grim. 'Technically, it does. As the oldest member of the ruling family, he has many responsibilities. But the constitution sets no limits on sensible delegation.'

'In other words, he likes being a one-man show.'

He nodded. 'Unfortunately, your idiom sums it up more accurately than anything in our language.

However, he will have me to reckon with if he does not follow the doctor's orders this time.'

Suddenly she knew why Philippe was so set on coming to Chalong. His presence was the one thing that could prevent Leon from overworking. The knowledge kindled an odd awareness inside her. From first meeting she had sensed that Philippe was a formidable enemy. Evidently he was also a formidable friend. Anyone trying to harm Leon would need to go through him first.

How would he perceive her attempt to talk Leon out of the marriage? She gave an involuntary shudder.

He misread the response. 'Do not concern yourself. Leon will be fine, with rest and care. But it means I shall be occupied with his duties as well as my own. I shan't have as much time to spend with you as I intended. There is much to see around Chalong. Will you be lonely with only Alec for company?'

She was caught off guard by a contrary feeling of disappointment. Surely she wasn't looking forward to Philippe's company? It made no sense, given her antipathy towards him. The disappointment must be at having to delay her talk with Leon, she decided. She could hardly burden him with her problems when he was unwell.

Her shoulders lifted in a calculated shrug. 'It's better than having to put on an act.'

He stiffened, taking a half-step towards her. 'You tempt me to test your acting ability here and now.'

Then his glance flickered to the aide, who was masking his interest in the tableau with some difficulty. 'Go for a walk. We shall...discuss this later.'

There was little doubt what form the discussion would take, and she was surprised at the rampant emotion the idea provoked. It was just as well the staff were on hand, she told herself—and almost believed it. The last thing she wanted was another of Philippe's demonstrations.

Fortunately—at least she told herself it was fortunate—he was too busy with state affairs over the next few days to make good his promise. Apart from mealtimes, she scarcely saw him at all, and even then he wore a distracted air. His eyes appeared deeper set than usual, and a frown was permanently etched into his forehead.

When she asked after Leon he assured her the older man was progressing well, although chafing at being forced to rest. It was clear that Philippe had taken over most of Leon's responsibilities as well as his own. She tried to shrug off an unaccustomed compassion for him. Shouldn't she be pleased that the extra work was keeping them apart?

So she was startled when Philippe joined her for dinner and announced that they were to attend a cultural event at the nearby village that evening.

'Are you sure you can spare the time?' she asked, hearing and not particularly liking the waspish note that crept into her voice. She seemed powerless to withhold it.

The tired way he shook his head made her regret it even more. 'I thought you understood why I'm neglecting you, Norah. Now that Leon is feeling better, it can be redressed, starting this evening. Of course, if you'd prefer not to accompany me...'

Alain and Kitma Montri had joined Philippe's party that morning. Was Philippe hoping Norah would refuse his invitation, giving him an excuse to invite the other woman? The prospect was unaccountably depressing. 'No, I'd like to come,' she found herself agreeing.

A carnival-like atmosphere prevailed in the village. A roped-off area had been set aside for the prince and his party, and his arrival caused great excitement, Norah noticed.

What did they make of her? She couldn't help wondering. She tried to act serenely confident, as she'd seen Kitma do, but it didn't help her inner turmoil. She just wasn't used to being the focus of all eyes wherever she went. Did one ever get used to it?

The performance was held in a natural amphitheatre against a backdrop of limestone cliffs shaggy with night-dark jungle. Spotlights picked out the performers and cast eerie giant shadows against the cliff.

A number of traditional songs and dances were followed by a shadow-puppet play performed against a backlit white cloth screen. Then came a dance-drama Philippe told her was called the Manorah.

'The heroine is called Norah,' he added, watching her face. 'Variations of it are told all through this region, although it is based on an Indian tale. The heroine is a heavenly bird who marries a human prince.'

A lump rose in Norah's throat. His eyes were in shadow, but there was a curiously caressing quality in his voice. 'She can't be called Norah. You're making it up,' she insisted.

He shook his head. 'Ask any of the others.'

A curious aching dryness claimed her throat. 'What happens to Norah and her prince?' she asked.

'She is forced to return to heaven, and he travels there to find her.'

'And the ending?'

He brought his mouth close to her ear. 'How would you like it to end, Norah?'

Something caught at her heart and tugged hard. 'Well, it's obvious he . . . he can't live in heaven and she . . . she couldn't live in . . . in his world.'

'Are you quite sure? Watch the performance.'

She tore her eyes away from him and tried to focus on the stage. The story was told in the form of a slow, sinuous dance, with the silent dancers dressed in elaborate beaded bird costumes. Their stylised, graceful gestures complimented the lyrics supplied by an off-stage chorus.

It wasn't until the chorus died away that she realised she still didn't know how it ended. She had been too busy relating herself to the heavenly bird,

Norah, and Philippe to the human prince. Damn him, it was just what he had intended, and her annoyance grew until she absorbed little of the succeeding performances.

By the time an intermission occurred she was seething with anger, recognising it was as much at herself for letting him affect her as at him for making the attempt.

She was sipping a cup of hot tea when a male voice called out, 'Norah? What the Sam Hill are you doing here?'

Beside her Philippe stiffened and Alec went on some kind of visible alert, his sharp eyes raking the crowd to pinpoint the voice. 'Robb?' she said in astonishment. 'Robb Penrose? It's all right, he's a friend from Australia,' she reassured Alec. Actually he was a photographer she'd worked with many times, but some imp of mischief stopped her from explaining that to Philippe, who stood tensely beside her.

Robb pushed his way through the crowd with another man and a woman in tow, a raven-haired beauty whose classical features tugged at Norah's memory. They looked a little shell-shocked when Norah formally introduced them to the prince. The woman recovered first and engaged Philippe in bright conversation.

Robb drew Norah aside. 'I heard you'd given up modelling but I'd no idea you'd reached such giddy heights. A prince, indeed. You *have* done well.'

'He's a friend, not some kind of investment.' She bristled, unreasonably angered by his tone. Just because his gorgeous companion had immediately moved in for the kill didn't mean Norah was the same.

Robb touched her arm. 'Cool it, okay? He's really something, so I can understand the attraction. And ruler of all he surveys, too. I'd better call off Jinny before she gets her claws in too deep.'

'Don't worry, Philippe can take care of himself.' With an effort she wrenched her gaze away from the two of them back to Robb. 'What are you doing in Sapphan?'

'We're shooting a calendar on the beach below the village. You're out of touch or you'd know that Jinny Stuyvesant's hot property right now. Her calendar's a sell-out in advance.'

'I'm not that far out of touch,' Norah said cynically. No wonder the model looked so familiar. 'How long are you staying?'

'Only two more days.' He dropped his voice. 'I don't suppose you could use your influence to let us see inside the royal compound? I hear it's quite spectacular.'

'It is.' She hesitated. Philippe was unlikely to approve. And did she really want Philippe to see more of Jinny Stuyvesant than was necessary? Jealous, she asked herself? The idea was absurd, wasn't it? She would do better to focus on the chance of escape that Robb's presence offered. It was a slim possibility but better than what she had at the moment. 'I don't need permission to invite my friends,' she said decisively. 'I'll arrange for you to come to lunch tomorrow.'

He grinned. 'Fantastic. Thanks, Norah, you're a pal.'

His arm was still draped around her shoulder when Philippe approached them, Jinny close behind. 'It's time we were getting back,' he stated.

She took a deep breath. 'I've invited Robb, Jinny and their crew to lunch at Chalong estate tomorrow. You said I should amuse myself while you're busy.'

The faintest flicker in his eyes telegraphed his annoyance, but his face remained impassive. 'As you wish, provided Leon is not disturbed.'

'You know I wouldn't disturb him.' She turned a bright smile on Robb. 'Come tomorrow at one. We'll talk over old times. It will be fun.'

Although Norah had issued the invitation, Jinny made an unsteady curtsey to Philippe. 'Thank you, Your Highness.' They'd all been drinking, Norah saw, Jinny most of all. Had Philippe noticed? For the first time she wondered if she was wise to invite them, knowing how Philippe felt about that part of her life. Then she hardened her heart. Maybe if he saw her with the crew, he would prevail on Leon to change his decision.

CHAPTER SEVEN

ON THE return journey to the estate Philippe was stonily silent. When they were finally alone in the chalet, sharing what had become a customary nightcap before retiring, Norah ventured, 'I hope you don't mind me inviting the photographic crew to lunch tomorrow?'

He set his jaw. 'They are your friends.'

They weren't, but she didn't say so. She'd worked with Robb Penrose, nothing more. She knew the type of crowd he and Jinny Stuyvesant hung out with. Their brand of hard drinking and living in the fast lane had never appealed to her, even when she worked in the same industry.

If it wasn't for the faint chance of escape they offered, she wouldn't have invited them at all. But Robb had said he was leaving Sapphan in a couple of days. If he could be persuaded to take her with them...

'Bedtime,' Philippe said so suddenly that she jumped.

'What?'

'You're almost asleep. Go to bed, Norah,' he said evenly. His gaze settled on the faint flush she felt rise to her cheeks. 'Or did you think I meant with me?'

'Of course not,' she denied a touch too fiercely. For a moment she *had* thought...

His hard look softened fleetingly. 'Much as I regret sending you to bed alone, I have work to do. I won't always be busy, I promise.'

She made herself sound flippant. 'In the meantime I'll be thankful for small mercies.'

His eyebrow lifted. 'More play-acting? You forget your audience.'

So this was how it felt to be read like a book. How had he come to know her so well in such a short time? It was all the more reason to get out of here. She didn't add *while she still could* even mentally, but there was a sense of it all the same.

What was going on here? She recalled reading about an empathy that developed between hostage and captor if the situation prevailed long enough. God, she wasn't going to let that happen to her. She stood up. 'Good night then, and thank you for the concert.'

He inclined his head. 'My pleasure.'

She fled towards her room, her heightened senses hearing the study door closed behind him. He spent most of his evenings working there. She was surprised he had allowed herself a few hours of relaxation tonight.

His bedroom was on the way to hers, and she paused outside his door. To escape with the photographic crew she would need her passport, which was still in Philippe's possession. Alec, the everpresent bodyguard, had retired soon after they re-

turned to the estate. Now was her best chance to
retrieve the document.

Still she hesitated on the threshold. This was his
private domain. Entering it felt like a violation. She
made her feet move. The room was timber-lined
and possessed a distinctly masculine ambience.
Judging from the piles of well-thumbed books on
every available surface, Philippe spent a lot of his
time at Chalong in this room.

One wall was taken up with closets and an intricately carved dresser. On top lay a leather folder.
She went to it. Framed photographs surrounded it,
and her eye was caught by them even as her shaking
fingers opened the folder. Her passport was there,
and she slipped it down the front of her dress, aware
of the hectic pounding of her heart.

'Looking for something?'

She let the folder close with a thump and spun
around, shock draining the colour from her face.
'I was just...'

Philippe crossed to her in swift strides. 'Yes,
Norah?' His voice was caressingly soft.

'I... your door was open and I saw the photos.
I came in to look at them.'

His hands slid along her shoulders. 'Was it only
the photos? Or is there a more compelling reason
for this nocturnal visit to my bedroom?'

Caught between a rock and a hard— She choked
off the metaphor even as it sprang to mind. How
was she to get out of this? 'Only the photos,' she
said firmly, wondering if he would read the hesi-

tation in her voice. *Was* there another reason for venturing into his domain, one she wasn't admitting even to herself? She rejected the thought as her gaze flicked to the photos. 'Your parents?' she asked with a note of desperation.

His eyes were unreadable for a moment before he allowed his hands to drop ever so slowly. As they skimmed her bare shoulders, her skin prickled with an awareness that weakened her knees and threatened her fragile composure.

She shuddered with relief when he picked up one of the framed pictures. 'Yes, they are.' His voice was tight with control.

They couldn't be anyone else. Philippe was the image of his father. Tall, commanding, athletic, projecting the same aura of raw masculinity even through the flatness of the photo. Beside him stood a delicate, fine-boned woman whose expression spoke of sunlit ease and grace.

'What happened to them?' she asked hoarsely.

He looked on some inner vision of darkness. 'Ten years ago a major earthquake hit Andaman, destroying half the city. I was away at Harvard. My parents were killed assisting the staff to safety when a massive aftershock rocked the palace.'

'They were together?'

'Always, and now—forever.'

For an instant a trace of pain glittered in his gold-flecked eyes. She felt an echo of it inside herself but quelled it by force of will. Know your enemy, she reminded herself. She could know him, even admire him, but if she let herself feel compassion for him she was lost. 'It must have been difficult for you to assume the throne under such circumstances,' she said stiffly.

He nodded. 'There was no time to mourn. The city was in flames and the people had lost their beloved king and queen. Apart from needing practical help, they needed a strong rallying point.'

In spite of herself she said, 'But you were only twenty-one and you'd lost your parents.'

His shoulders lifted marginally. 'My age and personal grief were not an issue. I had my duty.'

'So you returned and put your country back together.' *Who put you back together?* she wanted to ask, but set her teeth against the question. It would betray far too much interest in him.

She felt the interest stir despite her efforts to subdue it. When they first met, five years ago, his rule had been relatively new. The country was not only back on its feet but prospering. Those must have been hard years for him.

She drew a strangled breath, understanding suddenly what had not been apparent five years ago. The reason he had reacted so strongly at the apparent waste of her life. Those dear to him and many of his people had been deprived of that choice by the earthquake. Angry as she was at him for judging her, she could see and even understand his reasons. It didn't make him right, but it did make his stand comprehensible. She wasn't sure she liked that.

'Have you ever wanted to be other than—what you are?' she found herself asking. What was the matter with her? Having understanding forced upon her was one thing. Seeking it was quite another.

His strong features relaxed momentarily as if he found her question surprising. The question or the fact that she had asked it?

He shook his head. 'Some things are beyond individual choice.'

It was out before she could stop herself. 'But not individual desire?'

She met his eyes and caught something unfathomable in their depths. 'Desire can be controlled,' he said evenly.

As he was controlling his now? She wasn't sure where the certainty came from, but it poured through her and she reeled slightly. What a fool she had been to come willingly into his domain.

He caught her as she swayed, his grip firm on her bare arms, his touch like fire. 'You came to me,' he said hoarsely. 'I might almost be tempted to take your presence as acceptance of your situation.' His eyes bored into hers as he held her upright. 'But I'd be wrong, wouldn't I?'

The rapid rise and fall of her chest betrayed his effect on her. For one insane moment she wondered what it would be like to succumb to the arms holding her, to be crushed against the broad expanse of his chest and give in to whatever mindless pleasures followed.

Discovering how she had pushed his control to the limits gave her a heady sense of power. She felt an almost overwhelming urge to test the extent of that power.

He was about to be crowned the absolute ruler of his people. What gestures, words, touches would it take to rule him? The temptation to find out was as great as any she'd ever known. A groan slid from her lips.

He silenced it with a kiss so urgent and powerful it drove the breath from her body. She clung to him, her senses reeling, but she found herself returning his kiss with a fire that surprised her to the depths of her being. Of their own accord her lips parted and she tasted him in wonder. There was mastery here, but there was also giving of a kind she'd never before experienced.

She felt her mind split almost in two. The thinking, reasoning part urged her to stop before it got out of hand. The other part, the sensuous, wanton part Philippe had seen as the whole of her, insisted that it was *already* out of hand. That part didn't seem to mind that they were alone, late at night, with Philippe's ornately carved four-poster bed a few steps away.

Was Philippe right? Had she started to accept her situation? Or worse, even to enjoy her situation?

'No.' She forced the word out.

He stopped instantly, but his fingers traced a teasing line across the swollen contours of her mouth. 'No?' he echoed, his tone indolent. 'Are you quite sure?'

No, she wasn't sure, and the flush she felt staining her cheeks belied any denial she might make. Silence was the safest refuge, but he read the pulse beating frantically at her throat and knew even her silence lied.

He rested his fingers on the pulse throbbing in her neck to make his point, then trailed a leisurely line down her shoulder to the cleft between her breasts. Abruptly she remembered the passport hidden there and panicked, spinning away from him. 'I said no, and I mean it.'

His face darkened. 'I've never forced myself on a woman. Nor do I think I was forcing you this time.'

How could she blame him for what she had so blatantly invited? 'You weren't,' she said shortly.

'You sound afraid,' he said, his concern so apparent that she felt momentarily ashamed.

She *was* afraid, but only that he would discover the real reason she had invaded his room. By giving in to the throbbing needs he had aroused within her, she had allowed herself to forget about the passport. And she had thought she held power over him. Whatever there was paled beside what he did to her.

In her haste to get away, she had knocked over some of the photographs. To give her quivering senses a chance to recover, she bent to pick them up. Philippe took them from her without a word.

When she reached for the last one his hand closed over hers. 'You're trembling. You *are* afraid. Of me?'

She straightened, still clutching the photograph. He wouldn't accept less than the truth. 'No.'

'Of what, then?'

Of herself, she recognised. Of the awareness growing steadily that she *could* fall under his spell if she let herself. Let herself? She almost laughed aloud. There was no letting about it. His last kiss had been like falling into an abyss. One slip and the rest was inevitable. One didn't allow a fall. Once begun, it was inescapable.

'Maybe I'm trembling with desire,' she said recklessly, wondering if it was any wiser than the truth would have been.

His black look raked her. 'If you were, we wouldn't be standing here discussing it. We *weren't* discussing it a moment ago, until some thought intruded.' He became thoughtful. 'If you're worried about taking precautions, I would make sure you're protected.'

She recognised a wild urge to laugh as the beginnings of hysteria. She was worried about falling—and he thought she feared falling pregnant. The thought had never occurred to her, although it should have done. Her Alice in Wonderland sense returned, of being hopelessly out of control—and worse, of revelling in the feeling. Had she taken complete leave of her senses?

'As it happens, I am protected,' she admitted. On her doctor's advice she had been taking the pill regularly to correct a slight hormonal imbalance. She knew she should have explained fully as soon as she saw the thunder in his expression.

'Of course, you would be,' he said shortly, and she had a disturbing sense of having disappointed him yet again. She opened her mouth to explain then clamped it shut again. She didn't owe him any explanations. He was the one keeping her here.

She tried to add *against my will,* but the words rang false even in her thoughts. How much against her will were the last few minutes in his arms? 'It's late, I'd better go,' she said, unable to restrain a note of reluctance.

He held out his hand, palm upwards, confusing her, until she remembered the photograph still clutched in her hand like a lifeline.

She surrendered it, realising belatedly that it was a photograph of Kitma Montri. It was a studio portrait, artfully posed to enhance the woman's already lovely features and huge, almond-shaped eyes. She seemed to stare out of the picture in blatant invitation. That her own eyes had held a similar look moments before only served to make Norah feel worse. How could she have thought for a moment that there could be anything between her and Philippe when there was Kitma to consider?

'Only a prince could get away with making love to one woman in front of the photograph of another,' she snapped, unable to keep the hurt out of her voice.

His features remained carved in stone. 'Does it trouble you that I have her photograph here?'

What an admission *that* would be. Norah lifted her chin, striving for an equanimity she was far from feeling. 'Of course it doesn't. What I don't understand is why you don't simply marry Kitma, since you obviously want her.'

'You seem very sure of your facts.'

She gestured towards the portrait. 'Exhibit A. That isn't my photo you're holding.'

'Nor was it Kitma I was holding a moment ago.'

It was time for honesty, in some things, at least. 'Physical desire is one thing. I . . . I can't deny I felt it, too.' It was amazingly hard to admit, but something told her he was well aware of it already. 'But you can't build a lifetime on . . . on sexual chemistry.' It was the right thing to say, but she was getting awfully tired of the right thing. Even now her body ached with the need to be held by him, and yes, loved by him, and to hell with the right thing. 'Why don't you simply marry Kitma?' she asked in a soul-weary voice.

The stone mask slipped into place. 'Since you refuse to let the question alone, you may as well know that marriage between Kitma and any member of the royal family is out of the question. Under our laws, blood relatives, however distant, may not marry.'

Something stabbed her to the heart. Some part of her had been hoping he would say he hadn't married Kitma because he hadn't wanted to. But Norah knew she'd been right all along. He did want the other woman and was prevented by law from having her. So he would marry Leon's choice and have Kitma anyway, satisfying all the proprieties. She was astonished how much the realisation hurt.

'Can't you change laws?' she asked painfully.

'Some things are beyond individual choice,' he repeated with chilling finality.

But not beyond individual desires, she thought. Unspoken, the idea hung heavily between them. Thank goodness she hadn't given in to her own individual desires and allowed him to make love to her, she told herself bleakly. It would have been appallingly easy, she recognised. And appallingly wrong. She was still second best, in his estimation. Ideal to fill the role of consort. Ideal perhaps even in bed, when the real object of his desires was unavailable. But never first in his heart. The photo in his hands proved it even without his words of confirmation.

Closing her mouth on a sob of frustration, she turned and fled to her own room. The passport pressing against her breasts was cold comfort after the fiery hardness of Philippe's embrace. But it was more real and solid than his empty words of love. And with Robb Penrose's help, the passport would enable her to escape before she succumbed to Philippe's honeyed words and seductive touches.

Thinking of how close she'd come tonight made her more determined than ever to escape before it was too late.

She fell asleep refusing to consider that it might already be too late. All right, she wasn't entirely heart whole, she recognised. But neither was Philippe. It was some small comfort to know she had dented his armour a little, shaking his iron control beyond his expectations. No doubt it was a long time since any woman had said no to His Royal Highness. So why didn't she feel more triumphant?

CHAPTER EIGHT

SHE slept late. Not even the clamour of the cicadas, as loud and drilling as a fire alarm, disturbed her until mid-morning, when a maid served her coffee and pastries on the balcony that opened off her room. Prince Philippe was in conclave with Leon and would like to see her before her guests arrived for lunch, she was informed in the maid's softly musical English.

What did he want to see her about, she wondered, resting her palms on the wooden balcony railing and staring into a mass of creepers and foliage as tangled as windswept hair. Her bedroom seemed to be suspended above the rainforest floor like a treehouse, its wild beauty dangerously beguiling. A gilded cage, she reminded herself.

Even the thought of the camera crew's visit failed to cheer her as much as she thought it should. Wasn't she happy at the prospect of escaping from Sapphan? she asked herself as she dressed. Lost in thought, she jumped when the telephone rang.

'It's Robb Penrose,' the caller informed her. 'My stars, it's hard to get through to you. They guard you like royalty already.'

His humour grated on her nerves. 'What is it, Robb? Can't you make lunch after all?'

'Wouldn't miss it for the world. Not often I get to have lunch in a palace,' he said in the same maddeningly cheerful tones. He thought Chalong was a palace. What would he say if he glimpsed the real Pearl Palace at Andaman? 'I have a proposition for you,' he continued, 'although in your lofty position, you'll probably have me clapped in irons for suggesting it.'

She reined in her mounting impatience. 'I'm not royalty yet, so you're safe in asking a favour.'

He was suddenly all business. 'Good girl. Our make-up expert, Helen, is ill with some jungle bug and has to take it easy. Could you take over for her for the last day of the shoot?'

As a model and now a beauty therapist, she was more than competent for the job, as Robb well knew. It was so unexpected that she was silent for a long moment. Visions of Philippe's reaction filled her mind. 'I don't know.'

'It's only for half a day, as we leave tomorrow afternoon,' he persisted. 'Surely your prince can spare you from his harem for a few hours?'

Her back went rigid and her knuckles whitened around the phone. 'I'm not his property, so the decision is mine. I'll be happy to help out, all right?'

Robb heaved an audible sigh of relief. 'Great! I'll brief you over lunch and you can join us on location tomorrow morning. We fly out in the late afternoon.'

Not alone, if she had her way. Excitement grew within her, and a vague sense of something she refused to own as regret. She could hardly regret leaving after being a virtual prisoner here, could she?

Dismissing such thoughts, she finished dressing in a pale aqua linen suit, which showed off the light tan she'd acquired. She was surprised to find herself taking in the white leather belt a couple of notches. In spite of a fairly rich royal diet, she'd also managed to lose a few pounds. With her model height, she looked almost fragile. Contrarily, she wondered if Philippe had noticed.

He was waiting for her in the chalet he used as an office. Leon was there, too, and she was disturbed to see how thin and pale he looked. When she bent to kiss his cheek, he clasped her hands. 'You look charming, my dear. Philippe must be taking good care of you.'

Her glance flickered to the prince, seated at the head of the conference table, then to Leon. 'You're the one we should be taking better care of,' she reproved gently.

He smiled wanly. 'At my age all this pomp and ceremony take a toll, but it must be done. I'm glad you've forgiven me for not telling you everything I had in mind for you, Norah.'

'You should have told me. You can't spring a marriage on someone as if it was a surprise birthday party,' she said, but with no rancour in her voice.

His knowing look went from her to Philippe, and he chuckled. 'Ah, but it worked. You two are right for each other.'

He was seeing what he wanted to see, she thought, taking in the stone mask of Philippe's expression. Now if Kitma had been in the room ...

She drove the thought away as Philippe gestured for her to join them at the table. 'Leon believes it is time the people were formally introduced to their future queen,' he said flatly. His eyes gave no clue to his feelings.

Her own must be telegraphing her shock. They couldn't do this to her. 'But I ...' Words failed her.

'In two days I shall hold a conference at which you will be presented to our media, and through them to the people,' he went on as if she hadn't tried to speak. 'You will be taught some words of greeting in Sapphanese, but the rest of the conference will be held in English. I shall be at your side, of course.'

'Of course.' She lifted her head, and her eyes flashed a furious warning at him. How could he present this to her as a fait accompli in front of Leon, knowing she would do nothing to upset the already ailing elder statesman? It was a calculated choice, she thought angrily. Designed to gain her cooperation without a fight. Well, two could play this game. In two days' time, if all went well, she would be on her way back to Australia.

'If it's what you want, Your Highness,' she said with apparent capitulation.

Suspicion clouded his gaze. 'No objections, Norah?'

She smiled sweetly. 'None.' None she was prepared to voice in front of Leon, anyway. She stood up. 'If there's nothing more, I'd better prepare for my luncheon guests.' At the door she turned. 'There is a favour you can do for me, Philippe.'

His eyebrow lifted slightly. 'Yes?'

'One of the camera crew is ill. They've asked me to help out with the make-up tomorrow. I said I was sure you wouldn't mind. It will keep me occupied until the media conference.'

The implied bargain drove his eyebrows higher and he spread his hands wide. 'I can hardly say no, since you're being so cooperative about the conference.' *Later for the reckoning,* his look clearly stated.

She could afford to be gracious. 'Thank you, Philippe. Will you be joining us for lunch?'

He shook his head. 'I have other commitments.'

She found out what they were as soon as she stepped outside the conference room. Kitma Montri glided towards her on dancer's feet. Her cool gaze met Norah's flushed expression. 'You aren't coming with us this afternoon?'

So this was Philippe's commitment. No wonder he hadn't objected to Norah working with the film crew. It probably suited him admirably to have her out of harm's way. 'I have guests of my own,' she said sharply. 'Where are you going?'

Kitma smiled. 'To the pearl farm. Philippe wishes to choose some special coronation pieces.'

Her smug expression told Norah who would wear the pieces. She kept the hurt off her face as she bid Kitma a formal good day. When the conference room doors closed behind the other woman, Norah found her hands were shaking.

How dare Philippe humiliate her like this? In front of Leon he was all duty, planning Norah's introduction to the people, when he could hardly wait to escort Kitma on a jewellery-buying expedition.

She set her shoulders. Leaving with Robb and his crew had seemed furtive. In reality it was less underhand than Philippe's behaviour. Telling herself so didn't help as much as it should have done.

Lunch with Robb's crew was also less of a distraction than she'd hoped. The crew's awe of the regal surroundings and attentive service was soon overtaken by their typically Australian larrikinish sense of humour. Norah bore Robb's teasing about being a princess with as much grace as she could muster, but her thoughts kept returning to Philippe and Kitma. Was he choosing pearls for her? An image of him settling a pearl choker around the other woman's neck nagged at Norah.

'You haven't heard a word I've said,' Robb accused her.

She smiled apologetically. 'I have a lot on my mind lately.'

'But not so much that you can't work with us tomorrow?'

He looked relieved when she said, 'I'll be there.'

The conversation shifted to the calendar they were shooting and from there to various industry people Norah had known when she worked as a model. It was mostly gossip, some of Jinny's comments unashamedly malicious. Listening to them, Norah wondered if she had sounded as shallow and self-centred once. Was this the image Philippe had first gained of her? It was a sobering thought.

When the meal ended she took the crew on a tour of the estate, ending at a gallery used for formal receptions when the prince was at Chalong. Robb strolled among the artworks, exclaiming over the Klimt and the Chagall, the Gaudi and the Braque mosaics. 'This is really something.'

'It hardly compares to the Pearl Palace,' she told him, laughing. She winced as Jinny ran a careless hand down a centuries-old Greek statue in a niche. The woman had imbibed more than her share of wine during lunch, which seemed to be a habit, and was now floating in a comfortable haze. Norah hoped she wouldn't damage anything.

Moving to a console, Jinny picked up a doll-sized carving and peered at it. 'I bought one just like this,' she commented. 'It's supposed to be really old.'

Probably an imitation, Norah thought. The genuine article was beyond even a supermodel's salary. 'It's a Naga,' she quoted, remembering one of Philippe's lectures. 'The river spirit in the form of a serpent. It's carved from ivory by an eleventh-century school of sculptors who normally worked in stone, so it's quite unusual. There are only a handful in existence, most of them in Philippe's collection at the Pearl Palace. Are you sure yours is genuine?'

'I bought it through a friend of a friend,' Jinny confided, then giggled. 'They aren't supposed to be in private hands, and I paid enough for it to be the real thing.' She studied the sculptor's mark on the base. 'It has the same markings as this one.'

Robb looked uncomfortable. 'Then it may have been stolen from some gallery. Why do you always have to live so dangerously, Jinny?'

Norah's glance travelled between them. If Robb was in love with Jinny, it would explain his tolerance for the model's foibles. 'Maybe you should show the statue to Philippe for his opinion,' she suggested.

Jinny pouted. 'And risk having your prince confiscate it? No, thanks.' She smiled at Robb. 'Didn't you say something about a swim after lunch?'

He looked at Norah and shrugged. 'We've wrapped for the day, so I did suggest the beach. Like to join us?'

Her head ached and her nerves were tight with tension. She shook her head. 'I don't think so. Philippe will be back soon. I should be here.'

Jinny regarded her with sly curiosity. 'Is it true what they say about Sapphanese princes? That they're, you know, larger than life?'

Robb looked stunned. 'Jinny!'

The model's hands fluttered. 'I was only wondering.'

Norah felt her cheeks burn. 'I'm his house guest, not his mistress,' she said with a control she was far from feeling. She hadn't yet told them that Philippe already considered her his wife. If he had his way, it would be public knowledge within two days. Thankfully it wasn't yet.

Jinny nodded. 'I suppose that Montri woman could answer my question.'

'Kitma Montri is a member of Philippe's staff,' Norah pointed out. She felt sick. Was Philippe's preference obvious even to a visitor like Jinny? More than ever, she felt she was doing the right thing by leaving as soon as she could arrange it.

She was hardly conscious of Robb gathering up his crew and Jinny with an apologetic farewell. 'She'll be fine in the morning. She doesn't let anything interfere with her work,' he confided, gesturing towards the swaying model.

'It doesn't matter,' Norah said and meant it. Nothing Jinny had said was news to her. If anything, the model had strengthened her resolve to escape.

She paid attention as Robb repeated the arrangements for tomorrow's photographic shoot. Thankfully he was prepared to collect her from the estate. There would be no bodyguard in tow when she headed for the airport instead of returning to Chalong.

This time tomorrow she would be on her way to Australia. The thought should have cheered her. Instead she felt empty inside as she returned to Philippe's chalet to spend her last night under his roof.

Robb was as good as his word. A rented four-wheel-drive vehicle driven by one of his crew arrived to ferry her to the location early next morning. When she joined him for breakfast, Philippe accepted her explanation that her packed case contained professional make-up and equipment. It did, but it also contained a change of clothes and the bare necessities for a flight to Australia.

Still, when a servant came to tell her that the car was waiting, she hesitated. This was burning her bridges with a vengeance.

Philippe regarded her over his coffee cup. 'Is something the matter?'

Crazily, she realised she was waiting for him to say something, anything that would prevent her from going. 'Are you sure you don't mind me doing this job?' she asked, hearing the tremor in her voice.

'If I did, you would not be doing it,' he said with such assurance that defiance boiled up within her. Damn him, he did not control her. He was about to be crowned king, but he did not rule her. She was doing the right thing by putting as much distance between them as possible.

With her head high she swept out the door before he could think to order Alec to accompany her.

She was well aware of how late Philippe had returned last night. Too late to dine with her or share their customary nightcap. Kitma's company must have proved sufficiently diverting to keep him occupied well into the night.

Norah sighed, recognising her sadness as a disguise for the anger wrenching at her. He had no right to treat her as a convenience, dignifying his public role while he followed his heart in private. Even a king should have more consideration for the woman who lo— Loathed him. She completed the thought, feeling her face flame.

She leaned forward. 'Where is Robb shooting this morning?'

'The beaches and caves at Sunrise,' the driver said over his shoulder. Norah recognised him as Robb's lighting man.

There were two beaches below the ancient market town of Chalong—Sunrise and Sunset. Sunrise was the more scenic, edging a sheltered, curving bay. The water lapping the white sand was incredibly clear, while the fringe of coral reefs teemed with sea life.

Each morning the local fishermen staged an impromptu show when they fed leftovers from their catch to the sharks. Philippe had assured her the sharks were not dangerous. There had been no known cases of attack in the region.

It was not the fish-feeding ritual Robb wanted to capture on film. When Norah arrived, he and the crew were setting up their gear in the mouth of an immense cave festooned with theatrical stalactites and stalagmites, where, he told her, birds' nests were collected for processing and sale to the international gourmet food market.

She regarded the ancient cave paintings thrown into sharp relief on a far wall by the photographic lights. 'I can see why you decided to film here.'

'It was Hell's own job getting permission from the sea gypsies who own it,' Robb admitted. 'We can only have it for the one morning, to avoid disturbing the swallows who build the edible nests. That's why I left it till last. If we have any problems I already have enough footage from other locations to cover the calendar.'

Jinny was a different person this morning, bright-eyed and completely professional as Norah set up her gear and began transforming the model with make-up. The lighting was tricky, and the make-up demanded special care. 'I see you haven't lost your touch,' Robb said, admiring her handiwork.

After her work with scarred teenagers, Jinny's flawless complexion offered almost no challenge, but Norah didn't say so. Any doubts she harboured about the wisdom of giving up modelling had been dispelled by these couple of days in the company of Robb and his crew. It was as if her modelling career had belonged to a different person. Someone as shallow and self-centred as Philippe had accused her of being? It was galling to think so but hard to avoid.

Robb worked steadily for the next two hours, snapping Jinny against the cave paintings, beside an altar set up by the sea gypsies at the foot of an impressive stalagmite, and on one of the rickety bamboo ladders the gypsies used to harvest the birds' nests. While he changed film or cameras, Norah touched up Jinny's make-up so she would remain cool-looking under the baking lights.

Around mid-morning Robb called a halt. Jinny and the crew couldn't wait to escape from the cave to the sunlit beach beyond, but Norah caught Robb's arm. 'I need to ask a favour.'

He grinned. 'Name it, wonder woman. You got me out of a jam this morning, so I owe you a big one.'

It was going to be a big one, and she swallowed hard. 'I gather Helen isn't well enough to travel back with the group this afternoon.'

This much she'd learned from Jinny at lunch yesterday. Robb nodded confirmation. 'She's taking a week's leave and staying in Sapphan. Not a bad spot for R and R if you ask me.'

Norah wasn't sure she agreed. She ran a finger over her upper lip, noting the beads of perspiration gathered there. She was incredibly nervous. What if Robb turned her down or was unable to help? She took a deep breath. 'Could you possibly change Helen's air ticket into my name so I can fly back with you? I'll repay you, of course.'

He looked startled. 'Helen left it to me to cancel and rebook her flight, so it shouldn't be a problem.

What's the matter? Is the royal life-style wearing thin already? I thought you and the prince had a good thing going.'

She felt a driving need to share her burden with someone, and Robb was the nearest thing she had to a friend on Sapphan. She sagged against the cave wall, covering her face with her hands. 'Oh, Robb, if you only knew. Philippe wants me to *marry* him.'

His hands froze on the camera he'd started re-loading. 'And that's a problem? Sounds like every woman's fairytale to me.'

She let her hands drop. 'It isn't a fairytale, it's a nightmare.' She explained about Leon's right to choose the prince's bride. 'I have no idea why he chose me,' she finished on a tremulous note.

Robb's hand went to the side of her face in a gesture of comfort. 'Have you looked in a mirror lately? I'd say he's getting a bargain.'

'Philippe said the same thing,' she said shakily. 'But looks aren't everything.'

Robb frowned. 'Maybe he wasn't talking about looks any more than I am. Hell, looks are a dime a dozen in our business. But people like you, Norah, are a much rarer commodity.'

She looked at him, wide-eyed. 'What do you mean, people like me?'

'People with heart. Look at what you gave up to work with those injured kids. Not one woman in a thousand would have done it, but you did. And coming to my rescue this morning...' He silenced her with a finger on her lips as she started to contradict him. 'Don't tell me it was nothing. It meant a lot to me and Helen. She was worrying herself into more symptoms because she couldn't do her job. Have you considered these are some of the reasons your royal matchmaker chose you?'

She might have considered the possibility if not for one insurmountable obstacle—none of the qualities Robb named counted against the one she lacked. She wasn't Kitma Montri. 'Even if you're right, Philippe loves someone his laws won't let him marry,' she said after a long silence. 'I'm expected to keep her place warm for her.'

'Or the bed, in this case,' Robb quipped, then sobered when he caught her tormented expression. 'Sorry, it's no joking matter, is it? Hell of a thing to be a prince if you get your bride picked for you and she isn't your first choice.'

His choice of phrase slammed into Norah like a blow. 'Now do you see why I need to get away?' Tears trembled in her voice.

Hearing them, Robb set his camera down and opened his arms. 'Come here, kid. I've never kidnapped a princess before, but I'm game.' He held her tightly in a brotherly hug, which made up for a little of the loneliness of the last few days. 'We Aussies have to stick together,' he told her, running a hand under her eyes to dash away the tears. 'Better now?'

She managed a smile around the huge lump filling her throat. 'Yes, thanks. Or at least I will be when I'm on my way to Australia.' Funny, if she said it often enough and with enough conviction, she could start believing it.

There was a disturbance at the cave mouth, and Jinny stuck her head in. 'You have a visitor, Norah.'

Behind her loomed a dark figure, solid and commanding against the blinding daylight beyond. Even in silhouette it was impossible to mistake that formidable profile.

She jumped away from Robb as if stung. What was Philippe doing here? How much had he seen and misconstrued? In her panic, it barely occurred to her to wonder why she cared. Better if he did think she was promiscuous. One more reason not to insist on marrying her.

Even so, she recoiled from the coldness she saw in his expression. 'Philippe, I wasn't expecting you,' she whispered.

His dark eyes took in everything—the photographic set-up and Robb still standing close to her. 'Apparently not.'

Robb stepped protectively between them. 'Is there something I can do for you, Your Highness? Perhaps show you what we're doing here?'

Philippe's stone mask held. 'I hardly need a guide to tell me that.' He dismissed Robb with a gesture and turned to Norah. 'It was you I came to see.'

CHAPTER NINE

IN SPITE of herself, her nerves leapt at his entrance. It was as if an electric current had been switched on between them. She felt the surge of it sweeping across her skin, and the tiny hairs on the back of her neck rose in response. Try as she might to accept the feeling as a good thing, the hard accusation in his eyes cut her to her core.

For a moment she felt as guilty as if she *had* been doing something untoward with Robb, instead of accepting the simple comfort of his arms. Damn Philippe for making her feel this way.

Robb still hovered protectively, plainly unsure what he should do. Philippe was, after all, the country's ruler. Punching him in the nose was hardly an option, although Robb looked as if he was considering it.

She gave the photographer a shaky smile. 'It's all right, Robb. Philippe only wants to talk to me.'

The prince nodded stiffly to Robb, more in the manner of acknowledging a rival than paying a royal courtesy. She quelled an absurd sense of exhilaration. Philippe's behaviour couldn't amount to jealousy. He didn't care enough about her for that. It was probably the alpha male response to another of the breed. Not that Philippe needed to worry about Robb as a rival. That his kiss was more brotherly than seductive should have been obvious to anyone watching.

Evidently it wasn't. Philippe's voice was coldly controlled, his face a rigid mask as he stepped closer. 'Now I see why you were so anxious to undertake this assignment.'

Common sense demanded a denial, but her rioting emotions drove her to say, 'Why should you care what I do?'

For a fleeting moment she fantasised his answer—*Because I care about you.* But it would mean no more than the platitudes that Colin Wells had mouthed while keeping his wife and children in the background. In Philippe's case, Kitma owned his true allegiance. All the same Norah held her breath, wondering if he would say it and how she would feel if he did.

The fantasy was short-lived. 'I care because of your status,' he declared. 'You don't have the same freedoms as other women.'

'I don't have any freedom at all,' she snapped, annoyed with herself for letting his words hurt her when they were no more than she expected from him.

He gestured widely. 'Your presence here belies that. There are no bodyguards or other escort. You are hardly behind bars, Norah.'

'I may as well be. I can't leave, and it seems I can't act spontaneously around an old friend without causing an international incident.'

'You are not such a child that you can't tell the difference between a friendly act and throwing yourself into the arms of another man.'

Her control snapped. Around him she had little enough to begin with, but his accusation was the last straw. 'I did not throw myself into his arms,' she denied hotly. 'I was upset, and Robb comforted me. It's hardly a criminal act.'

His eyes narrowed, and his long fingers clenched at his sides. 'Why were you upset?'

Her lashes fluttered over blazing eyes. 'You of all people need to ask?'

Lowered eyes didn't stop her from feeling his gaze boring into her with laser-like intensity. 'Well, I can't damn you for your honesty. And I did ask.'

The cracking note in his voice brought her head up. For an instant he had sounded as if he regretted what he was doing to her. But his next words belied any such notion. 'I came to tell you I've arranged a tutor to coach you in the Sapphanese phrases you'll need for the media conference tomorrow. She'll arrive at Chalong later this afternoon.'

'Was it the only reason you came?'

There was a long pause. 'I thought it would be interesting to see you at work. It has certainly been that.'

His face was impassive as he turned on his heel. He was at the mouth of the cave before she rallied her confused thoughts and went after him. 'I won't be finished here until later today.' She flashed a look of appeal at Robb, who waited near the cave entrance. 'We still have more shots to take, don't we, Robb?'

Bless him. Robb picked up his cue, although he looked ill-at-ease. 'Er, yes, I want some shots of Jinny among those rice paddies out near Chalong airport. Can you spare Norah for a few hours longer, sir?'

Philippe's ironical glance raked Norah. 'Saying yes is preferable to having her rattle the bars of her cage at me all afternoon.' To Norah he added, 'I'll reschedule the tutorial.'

Before she could respond he gathered up his hovering entourage with a look and strode to the waiting cavalcade of cars. As they drove off, Robb slumped against a tree. 'Whew. You should have warned me that working with you would put me on a collision course with His Royal Highness.'

Her pain-filled eyes met his. 'I'm sorry, I didn't know this would happen.'

Robb's natural Australian ebullience asserted itself. 'Touchy customer, isn't he? Must be all that in-breeding.'

'It's nothing of the sort. Their laws prevent it,' she snapped, surprising herself with her vehemence. 'He's only doing a difficult job the best way he can.'

Robb looked stunned. 'Don't shoot the messenger. You're the one who can't wait to escape from the man, and now you're rushing to his defence. Are you sure you want to leave with us this afternoon? His Highness won't be happy about it, you know.'

She nodded, misery winding its way through her like a molten river. 'It's precisely why I can't stay,' she said.

The remainder of the shoot passed with agonizing slowness, or maybe it just seemed so to Norah's taut nerves. Jinny had started drinking during lunch, and her giggly behaviour further frayed Norah's nerves. How was she to survive a long flight with the model in this condition?

Somehow she got through the afternoon and the tortuous drive to the airport, which Philippe had pointed out on the way to Chalong. It was smaller than the main one at Andaman, but as long as it accommodated flights to Australia she didn't care.

Robb took charge of checking in the heavy photographic equipment boxes for which he had special permits and paperwork. He turned to Norah and Jinny. 'You'd better give me your gear, too.'

Norah handed him her bag so it could be weighed and tagged. Jinny, swaying slightly, clutched her bag tightly. 'I'll keep this with me.'

'It will have to go through the security check-point,' the attendant assured her, reaching for the bag.

There was a slight tussle and the bag tilted, spilling its contents onto the floor. Norah caught her breath as she spotted a familiar-looking carving amongst the debris of Jinny's personal possessions.

Jinny dropped to her knees and began to gather up her belongings, but the eagle-eyed attendant reached for the carving. 'What is this, madame?'

Jinny looked up blearily. 'It's only a souvenir. Give it back to me.'

The attendant studied the markings on the base and shook his head. 'I don't think so. You will all have to come with me while we straighten this out.'

Norah's heart sank. The last thing she needed was a fuss at the airport. The statue was the twin of the Nagas in Philippe's collection and, if genuine, was a national treasure and a prohibited export. Why did Jinny have to be so stupid?

Numbly she followed Robb and Jinny as they were taken to a small anteroom bare of all furnishings except for some hard-backed chairs and a wooden table. The only window was high and barred. Norah jumped as the door slammed behind them.

At the grating sound of a key turning in the lock, Robb whirled and tried the door. 'Bloody hell, they've locked us in.'

Jinny looked scared, as if her situation was finally penetrating her alcoholic haze. 'They can't put me in jail for carrying it, can they?' she asked in a small voice.

Robb glanced at his watch, 'I don't know, but whatever they do, I hope they do it soon or our flight will leave without us, and there isn't another until tomorrow.'

Norah's nerves were twisted into knots. She felt as if she was about to be sick, and swallowed hard. If they missed the flight, Philippe would find out where she was and stop her from leaving the country. She tucked her hands under her armpits and began to pace. What was keeping the officials? Why didn't they lecture Jinny or fine her and be done with it?

She started as the door opened to admit a man and a woman wearing the uniforms of airport security. The man's glance swept them critically, resting longest on Norah, who was visibly shaking, although she thrust her hands behind her back to conceal it. The man spoke to the woman in Sapphanese, and she came towards Norah.

'You seem unduly nervous. Why?'

Robb stepped forward. 'It's being locked in like this. We didn't know the blasted statue was real. Jinny here thought it was a copy.'

The woman's eyes never left Norah. 'I am no longer concerned about the statue. It is genuine and cannot be exported, as you must know by now. You will have to sign a statement as to where you obtained it, so we can track down whoever's handling these artifacts.'

'Then what's the problem, officers?'

'Nervous people invariably have something to hide,' the woman said, glaring at Norah, who felt the colour leave her face. 'Maybe we've stumbled onto something here. Perhaps the statue was a ruse to get us to overlook some other illegal activity.'

Norah swallowed hard, feeling her whole body start to tremble. If they found out who she was... She managed to shake her head. 'I have nothing to hide. You can search my bag if you like.'

The woman's expression hardened. 'Make no mistake, we shall. And we won't stop at your bag.'

'What do you mean?' In horror, Norah realised what the woman had in mind, and she recoiled instinctively. 'No, you can't do this.'

Over her shoulder the woman said something in Sapphanese to the man, and he came forward, pinning Norah's arms behind her back. Robb started to intervene but Norah said frantically, 'No, Robb. You'll only cause trouble for yourself by interfering. Catch your flight, I'll be all right.'

'But we can't just leave you.'

'Then call the Australian authorities before you go. Find someone who can help.'

'Count on it.'

Sheer cold terror clutched at her as she was hustled into an adjacent interview room. This one was clearly medical in purpose, with a screen, a hard narrow table covered by a sheet and a standard lamp that dazzled her eyes. 'Take your clothes off, all of them,' the female guard instructed, gesturing to the screen. Norah knew the other guard was waiting just beyond the locked door, and she shivered. There was nothing she could do but comply.

It was the most humiliating experience of her life. They were looking for drugs, the security guard informed her coldly. She seemed put out when she found nothing. 'I'm sure you're hiding something,' she said grimly. 'Perhaps an X-ray will show us the truth. Wait here until I come for you.'

Clutching the skimpy utility robe she'd been given around herself, Norah shivered with cold and shock. She could hardly accept what had just happened, far less consider what else might lie in store for her. Being nervous wasn't a crime, but she had heard stories of evidence being planted on suspects. It was all such a nightmare. When was it going to end?

She realised she was starting to accept her situation as hopeless. Her head came up. She'd done nothing wrong. Whatever they did to her, she must hang onto that. Maybe Robb had contacted the Australian consulate by now. There was a way out of any dilemma, if she could only stay strong until she found it.

Her courage almost deserted her when she heard the lock rattle, but she kept her head up. She was going to let them see she wasn't afraid because she was totally innocent.

Shock flooded through her in waves as she saw who had come through the door. 'Philippe,' she whispered, her throat closing on the name.

His eyes swept her trembling form, which was barely concealed by the thin robe, and steel glinted in the dark gaze. He snapped something Norah didn't understand at the hovering security people, and they scurried to retrieve Norah's clothes.

She hardly heard the woman's stammered apologies as she went behind the screen to dress. Moments before, they had been treating her like a criminal. Now, because Philippe was here, they couldn't do enough to make amends.

When she was dressed, Philippe took her arm and led her out of the interview room. Instead of returning to the main departure hall, they were escorted by fawning staff along a narrow passageway, which ended in a private exit directly onto the car park. It looked like the sort of exit used by VIPs to escape waiting crowds, Norah thought distractedly. Philippe had not addressed her directly since arriving at the airport. He must be furiously angry with her.

When they were safely in the car with Alec at the wheel, speeding along the road to Chalong, she let her head drop against the leather headrest. Whatever he did to her couldn't be worse than what she had just endured at the hands of the security guard.

'Are you hurt?' he asked in the long silence.

She kept her eyes closed. 'Only my pride.' Nevertheless he must hear the humiliation that vibrated in her voice, despite her efforts to conceal it.

'They were only doing their jobs,' he said in a clipped tone. She had never heard him so furiously angry. Was it with the guards for their treatment of her, or with her for attempting to run away? Probably both, she thought in a wash of misery.

'How did you know?' she forced herself to ask.

'Your friend called my office and explained what had happened. Luckily I was still in the area on business and could reach you quickly.'

Shocked by her arrest, Robb had probably done the first thing that came to mind. The consulate would have been simpler, she thought ruefully, but couldn't blame the photographer for his instinctive reaction. 'Is Robb all right?' she asked.

'He and his crew are on their way to Australia. I ordered the flight held for them,' he said flatly. 'The young lady's ''misunderstanding'' was resolved when she agreed to leave the artifact behind.'

His coldness finally broke through her restraint. 'Aren't you going to ask me what I was doing at the airport?' she finally demanded, tension coiling inside her like a living thing.

He turned his face aside. 'I know exactly what you were doing. Did you think I wouldn't notice that your passport was missing from my dresser?'

She whirled on him, her distress submerged in a flood of white-hot anger. 'You knew what I had planned all along? Then that pretty seduction scene last night was all an act. It meant nothing.' This time the hurt in her voice was all too real. She had come so close to giving herself to him last night that it hurt to find it was a ploy to give her enough rope to hang herself.

His hand closed around her chin, forcing her to look at him. 'It was no act, Norah. You're woman enough to know the difference. Why do you think

I wanted to kill those security people for laying a hand on you?'

The thought that he might actually care was enough to snap her remaining control. Despite her best efforts, tears spilled down her face, and she brought her hands up to hide them.

Instantly Philippe's arms came around her, unbelievably comforting, although she told herself she had no right to the comfort.

'Sssh. It's over now. Put it out of your mind,' he instructed in a voice that made the tears flow harder. Whatever she had expected from him, it wasn't compassion.

'It was h-horrible,' she stammered, drawing shuddering breaths to control the tears. She did not want to depend on him for anything, yet it was hard not to succumb to the temptation when it was being offered so readily.

A thought occurred to her that helped to dry her tears. 'If you knew what I planned, you could have stopped me at the cave this morning. You could have spared me that ordeal at the airport.'

'You can hardly hold me responsible for your friends' foolishness,' he pointed out. 'I can't govern effectively by bending the law to suit myself.'

If he could, he would be marrying Kitma instead of her, she thought furiously, not sure whether the anger was wholly at him for not intervening soon enough to save her from a humiliating experience or at herself for weakening in his arms just now. She straightened. 'What will you do now?'

He turned to her. 'What I should have done at the palace. Tonight you will rest after your ordeal, but tomorrow, after the formal announcement, I will take you as my wife.'

CHAPTER TEN

IN THE confines of the vehicle the air was suddenly too thin for comfort, and she found herself fighting for every breath. Her hand clawed at her throat.

Through a haze she was aware of Philippe rearing over her, working the buttons of her shirt until he had them open and coolness washed over her skin. 'It's only delayed reaction. Take slow, even breaths,' he instructed calmly as his face blurred above her. 'You are not going to faint on me now.'

By force of will and a lot of imagination, she held on to consciousness, somehow managing to ask, 'Why not? Because you order it?'

Her vision cleared, and she saw a faint smile playing around his mouth. 'No, because you aren't going to give me the satisfaction.'

Nothing else he could have said was more certain to rally her reserves of energy. If swooning at his feet would give him satisfaction, it was the last thing she would do. She'd recover if . . . if it killed her.

He saw the effort she summoned and nodded. 'That's better. You'll do.'

Her back stiffened and she caught a breath. 'As first aid, it's hardly state-of-the-art.'

His mocking gaze roved over her, coming to rest on her breasts, half-revealed by the undone buttons.

His vow to make her his wife after the media conference was restated in his taut expression. Just as well she had the near-faint to account for her rapid breathing. Otherwise he might mistake it as excitement, when it was the last thing she wanted to feel.

She resisted the urge to close the shirt. There was more to be seen on the beaches near Chalong. Let him see that she didn't give a damn what he saw — or thought about it.

'I assumed a challenge from me would have more effect than, say, smelling salts,' he informed her. Her thoughts were transparent to him, she saw from the slant of his mouth and flashing eyes. As if for emphasis he leaned forward and ever so slowly fastened the buttons of her shirt, letting his fingers trail across her burning skin with indolent ease.

Something caught at the back of her throat, and her fingers dug into the soft leather upholstery. The need to moisten her lips with her tongue was crushing, but would only betray his effect on her. Her traumatised state must be making her so vulnerable. Any other explanation didn't bear thinking about.

The gates of the royal estate loomed on either side of the car, and Philippe took his time straightening to accept the guard's salute with a casual nod.

She leaned back and closed her eyes. In a few minutes she could escape to her room at the chalet. It was ironic that she now considered it a sanctuary. But from what? Or was it more accurately from whom? She squeezed her eyes more tightly shut to avoid confronting the answer.

It was dark when Philippe assisted her from the car, and Norah frowned. Alec had parked the car in a place she didn't recognise. She tensed as Philippe's arm closed around her shoulder. She swayed on her feet when she first stood, but she could move under her own power, and her killing look told him so.

For an instant he removed his arm, but she sensed his hair-trigger reflexes remaining alert as she struggled to stay on her feet. When her knees gave way he braced her without comment, making it seem as if she was moving under her own steam.

'If you had tried to carry me, I'd have screamed the place down,' she said in a savage undertone.

He looked unperturbed. 'Precisely why I didn't propose it.'

He assisted her along an unfamiliar path, which she presumed was a back way to the chalet. Behind them she heard Alec drive off. The silence of the rainforest closed around them with startling suddenness.

It came to her belatedly that this was not the way to the chalets. In fact, they were nowhere she recognised. She straightened, fighting Philippe's arm, until she could look around. Behind them was a steep limestone escarpment shrouded in jungle. Ahead was the dark, phosphorus-deckled mass of the sea. In between loomed the bulk of a building, a log cabin, she saw on closer approach. She shot Philippe a look of alarm. 'Where are we?'

'At Chalong.'

'A long way from the rest of the compound.' Suspicion welled in her voice.

'This is my private retreat, where I come when I need to be alone.'

She was more disturbed than she cared to let him see. 'You mean there are no minders, servants, lackeys?'

'It's a myth that royalty is alone in the presence of servants. People are people. There are times when I don't want anyone around me, so I come here.'

She quelled a rising sense of unreality. 'But why bring me here?' She wasn't sure she wanted to hear the answer, or that she didn't suspect it already.

'We have not been alone since you came to Sapphan. I have decided it's time.'

Her eyes flashed shards of anger at him. 'You've decided? That makes it unanimous, does it, Your Highness? What you say goes. Well, not for me. I demand to be taken back to the chalet.'

'A few hours ago you couldn't wait to leave it,' he reminded her.

But she hadn't counted on being marooned with him in a private retreat, out of sight and sound of everyone. 'That was different,' she defended herself. 'It wasn't...'

'Out of the frying pan into the fire?' He completed the thought for her. 'Another of your useful Australian idioms, which fits the occasion.'

It certainly felt like the fire. His supportive arm burned through her light clothing like a brand, sending wildfire tearing along her nerve endings to implode somewhere in the region of her heart. It took a supreme effort not to turn her imagination loose on the possibilities of spending a night with this man in this place. The frying pan seemed positively safe by comparison.

'Frying pan or fire, neither has much appeal,' she said, not sure how truthfully. She regarded the looming bulk of the cabin ahead. 'Won't you be missed if you stay here? Is there a hotline or something?'

'Nothing you can use to your advantage,' he assured her. 'There is a hotline if needed, but my staff won't disturb us here short of a national disaster.'

Obviously her situation didn't qualify. She was in no fit state to tackle the rainforest in search of the chalets, even if she knew precisely in which direction to head. So she had little choice but to let Philippe escort her into the retreat.

Appearances could deceive. From the outside it looked like the simplest log structure. Inside was a modern dwelling divided into living and sleeping quarters by artfully carved room dividers. A small but well-equipped kitchen was separated from the living area by a breakfast bar. The only signs of royal patronage were the Rasada crest over the door, a discreet electronic alarm system and a bank of communications equipment partly visible behind doors in an alcove.

Philippe saw her looking at the alcove. He strode to it, closed the doors and locked them, pocketing the key.

She propped herself against the breakfast bar. 'Don't you trust me?'

His eyebrow canted upwards. 'Need you ask?'

Her sigh exploded between them. 'Why don't you just have me beaten for running away and be done with it?' She was tired of this cat-and-mouse game, especially of being the mouse.

He looked as if he was giving her rash suggestion an undue amount of consideration. 'Under our laws, it's a possibility, so I advise you not to try my patience too far.'

A shudder wracked her. What on earth was she doing, putting ideas into his head? Seeing his face, set with the effort of not laughing at her, she let anger replace her weakness. 'What about my patience? It's been sorely tried from the moment I came to Sapphan.'

His answering look was long and leisurely. 'From appearances, I would say the benefits outweigh any disadvantages. You have more colour, more vigour. One might almost say that opposing me is a beauty treatment where you're concerned.'

She tossed her head defiantly, warming under the casual but thorough scrutiny in spite of herself.

'Next I suppose you'll drag out the cliché about how lovely I look when I'm angry.'

He shook his head. 'It would be untrue. Anger cannot enhance perfection.'

She drew a sharp breath. She'd been a model for long enough to know her face wouldn't crack any mirrors, but no-one had ever called her perfect before. Especially not a man like Philippe, who was hardly given to empty compliments. She shook her head as if to clear it. 'Don't, please.'

He looked genuinely baffled. 'Don't what? You *are* beautiful, Norah. It is not a compliment but a statement of fact. Why should I not acknowledge it?'

Because she didn't want her simple anger confused by his honeyed words. His compliments only made her feel worse about running away. Justifying her actions to herself was simpler when she was fighting with him.

'Compliments may work with your other women, but I don't need them,' she denied hotly. 'It won't change how I feel about—all this.' Her gesture encompassed the room around them.

'It isn't intended to,' he said, his temper flaring. He directed a cutting look towards her. 'This isn't a battle, Norah. That was won the day you were chosen as my bride. All that remains to be argued out is the shape of our relationship, not its existence.'

His certainty was unsettling. Her gaze took in the simple cabin. 'Is this place supposed to set the tone of that relationship or sell me on the idea that royalty can be human, too?'

'Royalty *is* human,' he stated. 'Would you like me to show you just how human?'

She had the sense of a trap closing around her, and looked around frantically. 'There's no need to go to such lengths to convince me.' She was sure he had far different proof in mind, and was anxious to forestall any demonstrations. 'I'm sure all this rustic simplicity was set up by an army of staff who make themselves scarce before you cross the threshold.'

He frowned. 'As it happens, the only staff who come here are cleaners. There's no point in having a refuge from a palace if you bring the palace with you.'

She spread her hands wide. 'You can't help taking the palace with you, Philippe. As the absolute ruler of your country, you embody it wherever you go. Look at the way everyone jumps to attention if you so much as crook your little finger.'

He smiled, but there was a disturbing element of danger in it. 'You don't.'

Why did it always come back to this? 'Someone has to keep your feet on the ground,' she said a little recklessly.

His smile broadened to devastating effect. 'You see—Leon knew what he was doing when he chose you.'

A shiver shook her, but she suppressed the outward signs of it. He read her far too well already.

'Leon is eighty-one. He's entitled to a romantic ideal or two. I don't hold it against him.'

'But you do hold it against me?'

Her silence answered him as eloquently as words. He shrugged as if it was of no consequence. 'We'll spend the evening going over the phrases you'll need for tomorrow's conference,' he informed her, with a change of subject that disturbed her, much as she told herself she welcomed it.

She felt an unwelcome surge of disappointment. Was this his only purpose in bringing her here? 'I thought you arranged a tutor for me.'

'I have. And however much you might wish for another one, I will teach you what you need to know.'

What he might teach her didn't bear thinking about. She folded her arms in an unconsciously defensive posture. 'What will you do if I stand up at the conference and tell them how I was shanghaied into this role?'

He didn't blink. 'The conference is being broadcast by satellite to Australia. It is up to you what image is conveyed to your family and friends.' He came closer. 'I would, of course, follow such an announcement with one of my own, about the misconduct that led to your leaving Sapphan on your previous visit.'

'People have survived scandal before.'

'At what cost to themselves and their loved ones?' He shook his head. 'I don't think you wish to put yourself or your family through a trial by media.'

He was right, she didn't. But was the alternative, marrying Philippe Rasada, worth the price? The answer should have been a swift negative, but to her chagrin, she was no longer sure.

He smiled lazily. 'You see, already you wonder. What will it be like to be a princess, then a queen? To be beloved by millions. Being the bride of a prince has many compensations.' His voice fell to a husky whisper as he lifted a hand to her hair, letting the strands trickle through his fingers. 'Many compensations.'

'Perhaps I prefer being loved by one man rather than millions,' she said around a huge lump in her throat.

His fingers slid through the silken strands until he was cupping the back of her head. One touch and their mouths would be aligned. One touch . . .

'To a monarch, all things are possible,' he assured her. 'But your trembling tells me you are not yet ready for that one man. I have no doubt I could make it so, and I shall, but in good time. You are not yet fully recovered from your experience at the airport.'

He set her gently away from him. Striving for lightness and, she suspected, failing, she said, 'If all things are possible, what about room service? I haven't eaten for hours, and then only a sandwich with the camera crew.'

His look said he wasn't deceived by her change of subject. *Later for the real issue between us,* his eyes promised.

He gestured towards the kitchen. 'Since we have no staff, we are on our own.'

His effrontery restored some of her confidence. 'If I'm to be a princess, you can't expect me to cook.'

He was already moving behind the kitchen bench. 'I expect nothing from you that is not freely given.'

She had expected orders, arguments, anything but the discovery that he was more than capable of preparing a meal with his own hands.

In reluctant fascination she watched him assemble ingredients from the well-stocked cupboards and refrigerator. A large tureen of rice was set to steam, then he began to prepare shrimp, pork, shellfish and green leafy vegetables to add to noodles sizzling in a shallow pan. It looked like a traditional Sapphanese dish, and her mouth began to water.

He seemed pleased by her open astonishment. 'Cooking is a hobby,' he explained, 'although I get little chance to indulge in it, and then only for a few close people.'

It was out before she could stop it. 'Is Kitma Montri among them?'

His eyebrow lifted. 'Of course. She and I grew up together, so we are close.'

Knowing how close was unexpectedly troubling. 'And Alain, too?' she asked.

He nodded, adding ingredients to the spitting noodles. 'They were orphaned at an early age, so my parents practically brought Kitma up. Alain was

away at school much of the time, so we did not see
a lot of each other.'

He looked up from the steaming concoction.
'Alain interests you?'

She shuddered involuntarily, remembering. 'Not
in the least.'

'Such a strong reaction to someone you hardly
know. Or do you know him, Norah?'

What was he implying? He couldn't know that
it was Alain who had accosted her in the palace
gardens. 'We...met the last time I visited Sapphan,'
she said with difficulty.

His face tightened with disapproval. Of course
he would remember. His tone dropped to a level of
royal command. 'If you think to alienate me by
showing interest in Alain Montri, I would advise
you to think again. Nor is it wise for you to try
your wiles on him. After today you'll be under close
surveillance, as befits my future consort.'

She jolted to her feet. 'You mean you'll have me
watched? How long can you keep it up—a day, a
year, a lifetime?'

Her anger slid off him. 'As long as it takes to
convince you that I rule here.'

From anyone else such an assertion would have
sounded grandiose, especially in the setting of
kitchen and food preparation. But he managed to
sound both regal and terrifyingly authoritative. She
had the uncomfortable awareness that his status had
nothing to do with crowns and trappings. This was
a man born to rule, who carried his office and his

authority with awesome ease. For the first time she understood why kingship was believed for centuries to be a divine right.

A premonition gathered force inside her. This was the man who could rule her, and what was worse, he carried the knowledge easily.

The primitive flight-or-fight instinct goaded her to act, to challenge his mastery over her or to escape as far and as fast as she could. Neither was a viable option, although the chemical signals running riot through her body refused to recognise the fact.

She suspected Philippe was aware of her reactions, but rather than let him see the sudden weakening of her limbs, she dropped onto a huge saucer-shaped cane armchair, regretting it when the chair tilted her almost to a reclining position.

Struggling upright would have been even more undignified, so she remained where she was and projected defiance through her voice. 'I suppose this is retribution because I tried to run away?'

Abandoning the food preparations, he leaned over her, trapping her in the chair with a hand on either side of her body. She felt the heat emanating from him as waves washing over her. 'Retribution can take many forms,' he observed, 'not only the beating you suggested, or even imprisonment in an isolated cabin, but also in the form of almost unendurable pleasure.'

Her throat dried. 'Surely you can't—' she swallowed hard '—can't still want me after what I tried to do today?'

His face was impassive. Where was the anger he should be directing towards her? 'You did what you believed you had to do. Why do you think I permitted you access to your passport?'

It came to her in a rush of painful realisation. 'You wanted me to try.'

'To get it out of your system,' he agreed.

She had a fleeting memory of visiting a buffalo farm in Australia's Northern Territory. She'd been fascinated to see the huge, powerful beasts corralled behind fences of hessian and wire.

Not at first, she was told. When first rounded up from the wild, they were kept behind massive log fences, which they charged repeatedly in their efforts to escape. Once they'd tested the fences and they held, the beasts could be kept within more fragile barriers, because they had accepted their confinement.

Some of them even got to like it.

His looming presence was a far from fragile barrier, or she would have leapt out of the chair in protest against the very notion. At the same time, some part of her mind already saw the hessian walls.

She did stand up then, but only because he straightened and began to step back a pace. 'You're wrong if you think I'll ever stop fighting you,' she vowed.

There was no surprise in the glance he traded with her. 'I don't want you to stop fighting. Your passion makes you all the more desirable. I only intend to change the battlefield. Chasing after you could become tedious, especially as it's obvious you want to be caught.'

The hessian walls loomed. How could he be sure when she wasn't? Her confusion must have shown on her face because he grasped her wrist and began to pull her towards him, looking as if he would demonstrate his theory here and now.

She reacted on pure instinct. Moving in closer, she twisted his arm for leverage and reversed the hold into a forearm throw.

According to the self-defence instructor she'd gone to for training after her experience with Alain, brawn was less important than brains and agility on these occasions. She hadn't quite believed it— until Philippe landed heavily, cursing in Sapphanese.

His surprise was short-lived. She barely had time to absorb the enormity of what she had done. He was the prince, for goodness' sake. 'My God, I shouldn't have ... I didn't think ... are you hurt?' It all came out in a mortified rush.

Without warning he slashed out a leg and cut her legs from under her so she fell heavily on top of him. His powerful legs scissored across her body. She may as well have been set in concrete. His arms closed around her.

The glitter in his eyes told her she had made a colossal mistake, but not the one she was apologising for. 'Winded and surprised,' he said, sounding as if he was neither. 'It seems you have talents I didn't suspect.'

She squirmed in his grasp, but he rolled them both over and levered himself onto an elbow above her. 'I'm delighted you are able to defend yourself.'

Precious little good it had done her, she thought, vibrantly aware of every muscle and sinew of his body pressing her to the floor. Her repertoire owned no technique for defending against the riot of physical signals with which he threatened to over-whelm her.

His thumb and forefinger framed her chin, tilting her head up. 'No-one else on earth could have done what you just did and lived. Fortunately for you there are no bodyguards with hair-trigger reflexes to react to your treason.'

'Only you,' she whispered, afraid that was more than enough.

He nodded, his breath fragrant on her cheek. 'Only me, and as you see, I have a few moves of my own.' The pad of his thumb outlined the curve of her mouth. 'What would you have me do with you?'

Her heart was racing ridiculously fast, due to the throw and her fall, for it couldn't be reaction to his touch. His eyes were dark coals burning into her, into her very soul. What secrets could she possibly keep against that searching inspection? 'You could pardon me,' she said in a voice barely above a whisper.

His face was so close that she could see the faint shadow of a beard etched along his jawline. His teeth gleamed ferally against his glowing skin. 'Do you really want me to pardon you?' he growled.

She swallowed hard. Nothing less than the truth would suffice. 'No.'

He stroked the hair from her face, his weight braced on his elbow above her. 'Then tell me what you do want.'

The room swam around her. 'I want...I want....'

'Say it, Norah. I want you, and I know you want me.'

The words hovered on her lips, more true than even she had imagined. When had the fighting stopped and the wanting started? There was no clear line of demarcation she could pinpoint. It had happened so gradually that it was like a mist stealing over a valley, obscuring everything in its path.

She felt herself paling, knowing that once she said the words there was no going back. What would be left for her then, when everything she was and had belonged to him—and he belonged to Kitma?

She began to struggle in earnest. 'No, you're wrong.'

He gained his feet in a swift movement and pulled her to her knees, then all the way to her feet so she was moulded against him. She read mayhem in the hard set of his jaw, and for a blinding instant, his mouth fastened over hers, the kiss fiercely possessive.

Shock waves tore through her so she was still trembling when he set her away from him. 'Tomorrow,' he said in the voice of an order.

'Tomorrow there will be truth between us. Not only the truth your body was telling me just now, but the spoken truth, as well, which not only permits intimacy but demands it.'

'When hell freezes over,' she snapped, wishing she sounded more certain, especially to her own ears.

He heard the doubts and nodded as if in confirmation. 'Stranger things have happened. Can't you feel the chill breeze already? By tomorrow it will be a blizzard, I promise you.' He gave a low laugh. 'Why do you think I'm giving you so much warning?'

She knew, and couldn't conceal it from him. The anticipation had already begun to build. Knowing what he planned for her, the day ahead would pass with agonizing slowness while she imagined his possession many times over, her fantasies fuelled by this tantalising foretaste.

Even now every part of her yearned for his touch with a ferocity that was like hunger. Try as she might to subdue it, he had awakened a need in her that only he could satisfy, and he was well aware of it.

In her mind the hessian walls billowed around her.

How was she to get through the day ahead? How did one endure the unendurable?

CHAPTER ELEVEN

BY THE time Alec came to drive them to the chalets next morning, Norah was almost sick with nerves. Facing the audience at a major fashion show paled beside the performance Philippe expected of her. The phrases he had taught her after dinner last night swam through her mind as a meaningless jumble of letters.

But it wasn't the media assembling in the conference room that made her pulses pound. It was knowing that Philippe would come to her afterwards, and there would be no more time for talk.

She studied him through her lashes. He hadn't mentioned his promise again. Hadn't needed to. It had trembled in the balmy air between them last night as he coached her with surprising patience in his beautiful, musical language, and this morning as he served fruit, pastries and aromatic coffee.

He read her thoughts and took her hand. 'Relax, the people will love you.'

Not *I will love you,* just *the people.* They were the reason he was doing this, after all. Was he wishing Kitma could be at his side? Or would he banish even the thought as he did his duty?

She knew what the problem was. It had come to her in a rush as she lay in the dark last night trying

155

to sleep. Against all common sense she was falling in love with Philippe. The certainty had come to her when he rescued her at the airport yesterday, and was confirmed in her response to his embrace last night. Nothing else could explain the intensity of her feelings towards him.

A new possibility dazzled her. Philippe was about to proclaim her publicly as his consort. Her, Norah Kelsey, not Kitma Montri. Why hadn't she seen what unique power it would give her—the power to change everything if she so determined.

She could be the consort, in deed as well as in name.

She could be so beguiling that he forgot the existence of any other woman.

Excitement surged through her, but this time it was a positive charge. She sat up straighter.

Philippe favoured her with a curious look. 'Starting to feel better?'

She gave him a small, secret smile. 'Yes, I believe I am.'

With her new clarity of mind she was able to soak up the atmosphere around her. Helicopters beat the air overhead. Philippe had flown in the reporters rather than have them negotiate the steep pass leading into the valley, he informed her.

She was glad he had brought her by road, enabling her to enjoy the spectacular scenery and gain an insight into rural life in the island kingdom. Doubtless it was Philippe's intention. He did few things by accident.

When the car drew up beneath the portico of Philippe's chalet, he helped her out but paused at the entrance. 'I have business to attend to before the conference. You will be busy with your own preparations. We'll meet in Leon's study fifteen minutes beforehand.'

Direct. To the point. No reference to his plans for her. Yet they permeated his every action until she felt dizzy with the tension coiling so tightly inside her that there was room for almost nothing else.

As the door was held open for her, she turned for a last glimpse of Philippe to stiffen her new sense of resolve. He was going into a nearby chalet, and the woman opening the door for him was Kitma.

A pang shot through Norah. Was Kitma the business Philippe wanted to deal with before he announced his betrothal to Norah? Well, let him. After the official announcement everything would be different. Norah would be different. She already felt more serene, taller even, as if her life had gained a sense of purpose.

It had.

She intended to so captivate Philippe Rasada that he not only acknowledged her publicly as his consort, but privately, as well. Taking her to his retreat had achieved much more than either of them had imagined. She had glimpsed the man behind the crown, felt the power of his embrace and the heady anticipation of his possession. Now only one barrier remained. No matter what had precipitated it, this would be no marriage of convenience if Norah had anything to do with it.

She barely restrained herself while her attendants prepared her for the conference. A stunning Aloys Gada cascade dress in ivory taffeta with pearl fastenings was set out for her, and eager hands helped her into it.

The silky fabric whispering across her heated skin was a sensual reminder of what awaited after the conference, and she felt her colour heighten.

At the sight, the make-up artist shrieked in Sapphanese and began to fuss over her again, while a manicurist captured her hands for more attention.

Finally she was ready. Hastening to Leon's study, she felt like she was making an escape, although her confidence wavered at the sound of the reporters and camera crews gathering in the conference room. The sounds faded as she closed the door of Leon's study between them.

At first she thought he was late. Then she saw the frail legs protruding from behind his carved desk. She gasped as she leaned across the desk. 'Oh, no, Leon!'

Stifling the impulse to run for help, she dredged from her memory details of a St. John's Ambulance course she'd taken in her teens. Leon could be dying. Act first, then get help.

Panic gripped her, and she fought it, remembering enough to peel back one of the old man's eyelids. The pupil contracted immediately. Thank goodness he was still alive.

She heard the study door open and close again. 'What the devil...'

She knew her face was white as she met Philippe's startled eyes. 'I found him like this.'

The prince dropped to the floor beside Leon and placed his hand on the elder statesman's chest. 'No heartbeat. He isn't breathing. Do you know CPR?'

'I don't think...yes, I do.' It came back to her in a rush. Basic rescusitation techniques had been part of the course.

'Good. You'll have to breathe for him.'

His command snapped her out of her confusion. She knelt beside Leon's head as Philippe punched a red button located beneath the near edge of the desk.

'Emergency call button,' he said in answer to her questioning look. 'I had it installed when he became ill. Help will be here in a moment.'

He didn't waste even that moment. With an assurance that awed her, she watched him feel along Leon's chest until he located the breastbone. Then he closed his fist and thumped hard on Leon's chest.

Six times out of ten such a blow should have started the heart working, but her fingers still found no pulse. When she shook her head, Philippe straddled the older man and began a series of powerful thrusts that mimicked a heartbeat.

Some of his confidence transmitted itself to her, and her panic-fogged mind cleared. With only slight hesitation she tilted Leon's head back, pried his mouth open and checked that his airway was clear. Then she began to breathe for him, taking great gasping breaths due to her own panic. She prayed it was enough.

Between breaths she saw perspiration flow down Philippe's face. He didn't pause, didn't lessen the pressure of the relentless thrusts, but his expression was fierce. 'This is taking too long. Where the hell's that doctor?'

She had no breath to answer, but her heart swelled at the reassurance Philippe radiated. As long as he was with her, everything would be all right. He wasn't a doctor, but he had known exactly what to do. She could feel him willing Leon to live, infusing the older man with his own life force.

Only minutes had passed, but they felt like hours in the timelessness created by the crisis. As she worked alongside Philippe an intimacy linked them beyond anything she'd ever known. It was the closeness of comrades in arms, of firefighters at a fire front, of those who battled in the arenas of life and death. Sometime she would have to examine this bond, which was so precious, yet so crisis-forged as to feel like steel. For now there was work to do.

Growing light-headed with the effort of breathing for Leon, she was dimly aware of a commotion around them. Finally someone had responded to Philippe's call. He was grim-faced about that, his look saying someone would answer for it later. For now he threw orders over his shoulder, never pausing in his lifesaving efforts.

At last the medical team rushed in and moved them aside. Norah swayed on her feet and Philippe steadied her with a strong arm around her shoulders.

'He's in good hands now. You can relax.'

'What happened?'

'It looks like a stroke. The doctor's been nagging him about his blood pressure for days, and he's been having bad headaches and numbness in his arm. Apparently they're warning signs.' His mouth twisted. 'Not that Leon could be persuaded to take any notice.'

'Philippe...' He caught her as she sagged, then all but carried her to a nearby couch. 'I'm all right, just a little dizzy,' she insisted.

'You've every right. You probably saved his life.'

'Not me. You did most of the work.'

He smiled tautly. 'Let's not argue the point. Rest until the dizziness passes.'

It had already passed, but she stayed where she was, loath to lose the comfort of his hand on her shoulder. 'What happens now?'

He glanced at the medical team working over Leon. 'As soon as he's stable I'll have him flown to the hospital in Andaman, where he'll get the best of care. The helicopter is already on standby.'

She looked at him in astonishment, although she shouldn't be surprised any more by the speed and efficiency with which he got things done. 'Can he travel in an ordinary helicopter?'

He gave her a wry look. 'It isn't an ordinary helicopter. It's my own, designed to function as a flying ambulance if needed.'

A vision of the terrorist attack on his family's plane rose up to haunt her. The nearness of the medical team should have been reminder enough, but she hadn't thought. . . .

He read the fear in her eyes and tightened his grip on her. 'Hazard of the job, I'm afraid.'

But dear lord, always to be a hair's-breadth away from death from any number of causes! Could she live with knowing that his position put him eternally at risk in a world of terrorists and fanatics?

Her head came up. He lived with it, so she would. She had made her commitment privately and had no intentions of changing it, even though Philippe still didn't know how she felt. With Leon's life in the balance, it wasn't the time. Later would do. They would have a lifetime of laters. She could afford the luxury of waiting.

She watched numbly as the doctors hooked Leon to a battery of life-support equipment and took him to the helicopter, whose rotors throbbed in readiness on the landing pad in the centre of the compound. Philippe had elected to travel with them.

'Alain will make an announcement to the media,' he told her. 'Then he'll bring you to Andaman by chopper. Will you be all right?'

The thought of being apart from him tore at her, but she managed a nod. 'You go. I'll be fine.'

He had worries enough without adding her own. She was rewarded when his face cleared. 'Good. I'll see you at the hospital. I've sent a message to Talay's school. She'll want to be with Leon, too.'

Norah's heart went out to the teenager who'd returned to school so confidently such a short time before. Having lost her parents, it would be a cruel blow if she lost her grandfather, as well. 'Poor Talay,' she whispered, her heart aching.

His eyes showed that he understood, and he gripped her shoulders. 'You were good for her before. She'll need your strength again today.'

'I'll do what I can,' she said through the mist fogging her vision. By the time it had cleared, the helicopter was lifting off.

She felt bone-weary by the time another helicopter was fuelled and ready to return her to Andaman. The reporters had already begun to disperse, carrying the news of Leon's collapse in lieu of the story they'd come for. The elder statesman was a much-loved figure, and soon all of Sapphan would be holding its collective breath and praying for his recovery.

Norah was strapping herself in when Alain Montri bounded aboard the helicopter and took the seat beside her. The craft was an executive model with every luxury, including soundproofing, which enabled them to talk in relative comfort as the rotors churned the air towards the capital.

'Isn't Kitma coming with us?' she asked, noting the empty seat beside him.

He gave a sly smile. 'She went with Philippe in the first chopper. The way things are between them, he needed her comfort. You know she's much better suited to him than—let's face it—than an outsider.'

Norah's heart gave a lurch. 'I wouldn't have been an outsider after the media conference, would I?'

'But the conference was cancelled, and probably for the best.' He leaned forward. 'You don't belong here. You don't know our customs, our language.'

He was only voicing the doubts that had plagued her as recently as yesterday. But this was Alain Montri, the last man on earth she should allow to influence her. His very presence made her flesh crawl. 'Stop it,' she insisted. 'Aren't you worried that I'll tell Philippe what you tried to do to me five years ago?'

He gave a harsh laugh. 'He wouldn't believe it if you told him.'

Her fingers tightened around the seat belt. 'You seem very sure.'

He reached for her chin, pulling her face around although she tried to jerk away. 'I'm sure, because I have witnesses who'll swear I was nowhere near you after the reception. You can't win. You're out of your league here. Go home to Australia.'

Not long ago she would gladly have done so. Now it meant leaving the man she loved. It would tear her heart out. 'The choice isn't mine to make,' she said hoarsely.

Alain's eyes flashed with contempt. 'Don't tell me you've fallen in love with Philippe. That's it, isn't it?'

Her temper sparked. The feeling was too new and tender to stand inspection, especially from someone as contemptible as Alain. 'It's none of your—'

'You *have* fallen for him,' he cut in. 'Or is it the idea of being a queen with all of Sapphan at your feet?'

Her chin lifted. 'Being a queen has nothing to do with how I feel about Philippe.'

Alain's disgusted look raked her. 'Then you're a bigger fool than I thought. At least a motive like greed I could understand.'

'You would,' she snapped.

He shook his head. 'Being royal isn't about fairytales and romance. It's about politics and power.'

'Not to Philippe. He cares about his people.'

His hand slashed the air. 'Then he's a fool, too. This country could be one of the wealthiest in the region if we exploited more of our minerals and natural resources. Instead we settle for pearls and pretty scenery.'

It was impossible to conceal her shock. Alain was one of Philippe's closest aides. Did the prince know about these sentiments? 'How do you know I won't tell Philippe what you've told me?' she asked shakily.

He grinned mirthlessly. 'Because I'll deny it and accuse you of sowing discord. After your bungled escape attempt, he's suspicious enough to believe me.'

She took a breath, recognising it as truth. Then another thought occurred to her. 'Did you tamper with Leon's emergency call button?'

'You noticed how long it took the cavalry to arrive? Well, maybe the odd wire worked loose. Accidents happen.'

And could be made to happen. She went cold from head to foot thinking of how far Alain was prepared to go to achieve his ends. 'You'll stop at nothing to get rid of me,' she said in horror.

'Politics and power,' he reminded her. 'You see why you don't fit in? Your kind plays by the rules while mine takes the game out from under your nose.'

There was no more time to argue. The helicopter set them down in the grounds of the Pearl Palace, where Talay was waiting. White-faced and trembling, she came to Norah with a cry of distress. 'He's going to die, isn't he?'

'We don't know, sweetheart. The doctors are doing everything they can for your grandfather. I'm to take you to him right away.'

Never was she so grateful for royal privilege, which cleared their path like magic through the congested streets. They reached the hospital in minutes and were ushered to a fifth-floor lounge, which had been set aside for Philippe's exclusive use. Norah was barely aware of the luxurious surroundings as Talay flew to the prince. 'Uncle

Philippe, Norah told me you saved Grandfather's life. You're wonderful.'

For once Philippe looked nonplussed. 'Norah had a little to do with it herself. I don't suppose she mentioned that?'

His glance over Talay's dark head took in Norah's blushing demurral. 'How is Leon?'

Talay tensed in her uncle's arms as he said, 'He's holding his own. They have him on oxygen but he hasn't regained consciousness yet.'

Talay gave a sob. 'If he dies I'll have no-one.'

Instinctively Norah reached for the girl. 'You have Uncle Philippe. He'll always be here for you.'

The teenager turned moist eyes to Norah. 'Will I have you, too?'

She felt Philippe's eyes on her as she took a breath. 'Me, too,' she said firmly. Nothing Alain could do or say could change how she felt about Philippe. They were in this together, for better or worse.

At Talay's pleading, a nurse took her in to see her grandfather, and Norah was finally alone with Philippe. The silence between them was almost palpable. 'That was a touching performance,' he said.

She whirled, confused. 'What do you mean?'

He folded his arms across his broad chest, the stone mask firmly in place. 'Wouldn't it suit you if Leon didn't make it? He got you into this, after all.'

'Nevertheless, I care about him. I don't want him to die.'

'Aren't you going to ask who nominates my bride if he does die?'

She could hardly force the word out. 'Who?'

'I do.'

Was he waiting for her to ask whom he would choose? She refused to humiliate herself by asking. She was afraid to hear the answer, she realized. One more day and the choice would have been binding. Leon's collapse had changed everything. Philippe had called her his wife, but...

'What happens if two people—change their minds about wanting to marry after they make the commitment?' She forced herself to ask the question. This at least she must know.

His smile taunted her. 'Trying to tell me you've changed your mind, Norah? It's fair enough, I suppose, since you weren't given a choice in the first place.'

He racked long fingers through his hair, tousling it. He looked suddenly older and wearier. 'The question is academic while Leon lives. Go back to the palace with Talay. There's nothing more you can do here, and you'll be told any news. But for Talay's sake, at least keep your true feelings to yourself if the news is bad.'

How could he think so poorly of her? She felt sick with misery as she accompanied Talay to the palace, persuaded her to eat a little supper then sat beside her until she fell into an exhausted sleep.

She should go to bed herself. God knew every bone ached with tiredness. But she knew she wouldn't rest until Philippe returned. The possibility that Alain had tampered with Leon's emergency call button haunted her until she reached a decision. Whether Philippe believed her or not, he should be told. She would never forgive herself if anything worse happened through her inaction.

She waited for him in an anteroom where he invariably spent part of each evening. But she must have dozed off in the comfortable wing chair. She awoke to the sound of voices. Philippe was back, but he had brought Kitma Montri with him.

They couldn't see her over the tall chair, and Kitma's voice floated across to her. 'Oh, Philippe, everything will be different now. I'm trying to tell myself it's for the best but...' Her voice tailed off in a sob, and Norah saw Philippe take the woman in his arms.

Noah recoiled as if from a blow. Dear lord, Leon must have died. That's why Kitma was saying everything would be different. They moved off, and Norah fled to her suite, feeling as if her world had come to an end.

Her heart ached for dear Leon, who had only tried to do what he thought was best. Now Norah would get her wish and be sent back to Australia. Except that all she wanted was to stay with Philippe.

Needing the solace of activity, she began blindly to pile clothes into a suitcase. Philippe wouldn't want her around now. *Everything would be different.*

She started with shock when he came into the room as if conjured out of her whirling thoughts. He took in the scene at a glance. 'You couldn't wait, could you?'

'There's nothing for me to wait for. I heard you and Kitma talking and—'

'And decided you were off the hook. I saw you sneaking out of the room, but if you'd waited a few minutes longer you'd have heard the rest. The doctors expect Leon to recover, but there will be a degree of impairment. He'll have to restructure his life-style, reduce his public commitments.'

That was what would be different? 'You mean he isn't . . .' She couldn't force the words out.

'Sorry if it disappoints you, but he's going to live.' He moved toward her, and the air was suddenly supercharged with the aura of his nearness. She could hardly think straight. He had thought she welcomed Leon's passing as a reprieve. How could he think such a thing of her?

His hand closed over her wrist, and he spun her to face him. 'Why were you waiting up for me?'

'I'm sure you can think of some unflattering explanation that fits your preconceptions.' She threw the words at him, her voice cracking with emotion.

'I'd rather hear the truth.'

She took a deep breath. It was too late to change his opinion of her, but she couldn't live with herself if she didn't tell him what she knew. 'Leon's emergency call button was tampered with to delay summoning help.'

He nodded as if the news came as no surprise.
'Alain told me after I ordered an investigation into
why the call system failed. He said you boasted of
getting a worker to do it for you in order to get
Leon out of the way. Alain didn't want to tell me,
but he was afraid he'd be suspected, since it also
left the field clear for Kitma.'

Her eyes widened with horror. 'You can't believe
I'd do such a thing? I tried to save Leon.'

'You could hardly do less after I walked in on
you.' His hard expression fractured marginally.
'Norah, I don't want to believe this of you.'

'Then don't,' she pleaded, agony firing along
every nerve. Having him think she could do this
hurt beyond anything she'd ever imagined. 'You
only have Alain's word against mine, and he told
you himself that *he* has something to gain from
hurting Leon.'

Philippe looked grim. 'I know. For Leon's sake,
I want answers, and I intend to have them. So don't
finish packing just yet.'

He walked out, and she was alone. Alone and in
love with a man who suspected her of such evil.
The night that had held such promise now seemed
utterly black and endless. A long, dark night of the
soul. Beyond her window a night-bird keened
in sympathy.

CHAPTER TWELVE

NORAH heaved a sigh of relief as the palace gates closed behind the limousine, cutting them off from the clamouring journalists and photographers outside. She was trembling. 'I can't believe they followed us all the way from the hospital. What do they want?'

Talay smiled. 'Haven't you read the newspapers? Of course, you don't read Sapphanese yet, although your conversation is improving.'

'I'm trying.' Pointless though it seemed now, she used every opportunity to learn new words and improve her pronunciation. It was sweet of Talay to notice, and she said so.

The teenager grinned. 'I'm not the only one. The papers are calling you a mystery woman and asking about your role in Philippe's life.'

She was asking herself the same thing. 'Have they drawn any conclusions?'

'They expect Uncle Philippe to announce his betrothal before the coronation, and they've decided you're it.'

Norah compressed her lips. 'Oh, no.'

Talay leaned forwards. '*Are* you in love with Uncle Philippe?'

'Yes,' Norah said with an effort. She had a feeling she was transparent to the teenager, anyway.

'Then what's the problem?'

The problem was the one-sided nature of the relationship. Since returning to the capital, the prince had been much more distant towards her. She told herself it was the strain of Leon's illness coupled with the extra burdens imposed on Philippe, but the real reason was obvious. After Alain's accusations, Philippe didn't care to be around her.

If Leon recovered, Philippe would marry her, as custom demanded, but the prospect held no joy for Norah. Whether he changed the law to allow him to marry Kitma later on, or kept Norah as his wife while pursuing his real love, didn't matter. Either way, he was lost to Norah.

Talay touched her hand. 'Why do you look so sad? Is it because of Grandfather?'

Norah smiled wanly. 'It is hard to see him in a coma for—what is it?—three days now. But the doctors are optimistic, so we should be, too.'

Talay nodded. 'You didn't give up on me when I was sick. And you won't give up on Vana till she's better, too.'

This time Norah's smile was warm. Vana was Talay's school friend, who had been badly burned when she overturned boiling water on herself. When Talay asked Norah to try to help, she readily agreed. She had little enough to do at the palace.

Like Talay, the teenager was withdrawn and bitter about her disfigurement. When Vana saw what could be done with therapeutic cosmetics, skilfully applied, the shell she'd built around herself began to crack open.

Now the hospital staff wanted Norah to use her skills to help other patients. But Norah hesitated, unsure of her future in Sapphan or if Philippe would approve of her activities.

There was only one way to find out. It wasn't a convenient excuse to see him, she told herself. It had nothing to do with the yawning chasm created by his indifference.

When she asked his secretary for an appointment, Philippe surprised her by inviting her to lunch. 'I wasn't sure you'd be able to spare the time,' she said diffidently.

'You are my wife,' he pointed out. 'You need no appointment to see me.'

No matter what Sapphanese law said, she didn't feel in the least married, and she felt a blush starting as she considered why. Theirs was a contract that could still be broken by mutual agreement. She now knew enough Sapphanese law to know that.

She stirred the spicy tomato consommé without tasting it. 'There's something I need to ask you.'

His gaze swept over her. 'Yes, Norah?'

She wished he wouldn't look at her so—so possessively, as if there was more between them than she knew existed. It made marshalling her thoughts almost impossible. She managed it with an effort and explained about helping Talay's friend at the hospital. 'Her morale took a giant leap after she saw what a little make-up could do,' she finished, slightly breathless. 'Others in the same predicament want my help but I felt I should ask you before I agreed to anything.'

At her defensive tone he arched an eyebrow. 'Did you doubt that I would agree?'

'Well, I didn't...'

'What kind of ogre do you think I am?' he pressed on. 'I know that time hangs heavily on your hands while I'm busy, so I'm pleased you can occupy your time and talents in such a worthwhile way.'

Of course he would agree. Why hadn't she thought of it before? The busier Norah was, the more time he would have to spend with Kitma. The woman had apparently taken over some of Leon's work for the coronation, and spent a good deal of time in conference with Philippe.

A waiter took away her untouched soup and served a course of curried crab steamed with vegetables and served in a banana-leaf cup. She picked at it, unable to summon much appetite although the aroma was succulent enough.

Philippe frowned as she played with her food. Finally he asked, 'Has Kitma spoken to you about the Festival of Lights?'

The other woman had discussed it with Norah the day before. It was one of the country's most important festivals, marking the prince's birthday. No matter when his actual birthdate, traditionally the Festival of Lights affirmed his importance to the people.

'Will it still take place while Leon's in hospital?' she asked.

His eyes flamed with some banked-up inner fire of resolution. 'It's precisely because of Leon's condition that the festival will go ahead.'

A shudder shook her as love for this man flowed through her. He looked as if he could stand alone against the forces of chaos—and prevail. If only the gulf between them wasn't so vast. 'I don't understand,' she ventured. 'Leon's illness has nothing to do with—'

'Doesn't it?' he interrupted ruthlessly, forcibly reminding her that she was suspected of plotting against Leon. It was a sickening thought. He went on, overriding her thoughts. 'If Leon's emergency call button hadn't been tampered with, he would have received medical help sooner. It could have made a difference. I'll never know. But I do know that after the terrorist attack and now Leon's illness, I must create a sense of business as usual to allay people's fears. Part of the festival involves writing down your deepest hopes and setting them upon the waters for fate to read. Who knows, it may even help.'

It would take more than launching her hopes aboard a paper boat to make them come true, she thought bleakly. But she of all people knew the importance of symbolism. The cosmetic help she gave to damaged teenagers wasn't therapeutic. It did no medical good. But as a symbolic restoration of what they had lost—their beautiful outer selves—it was effective. Maybe crystallising one's hopes and

dreams in some form helped the individual to focus
on them, bringing them closer to reality.

She was willing to try anything.

'What do I have to do?' she asked.

'You will be at my side as I launch the festival,'
he told her.

'Will anyone know who I am and why I'm with
you?'

He allowed a taut smile to register on his even
features. 'I think they will guess.'

Of course, the newspapers. It seemed Philippe
was content to let them speculate. He had said
nothing about an official announcement since they
returned from Chalong.

At least one of her hopes was realised before the
festival began two days later.

'Leon is out of his coma,' Philippe announced
when he came to fetch her.

The elder statesman had been stirring when she
visited him a few hours before. 'That's wonderful.'
She choked on the words. 'How is he?'

'His left side is weak and his speech is affected,'
he told her, 'but he can make himself understood.
He should regain more speech as he recovers.' He
paused. 'He is pleased the festival is going ahead.'

Something in Philippe's manner stopped her in
her tracks. He wasn't telling her everything. 'Are
you sure he's all right?' she probed.

Even as she asked the question, the answer presented itself. Leon's recovery meant his choice of
Philippe's bride would stand. No wonder Philippe
looked so icily controlled, as if he would like to do

murder. Norah shivered. He looked capable of just about anything.

But there was no time to discuss it. The streets of the capital were thronged with people who had turned out for the popular festival. It was sunset, and the sky turned to gold as the royal procession wended its way through the gates, attended by a phalanx of police on motorcycles. The noise was deafening.

Nearly all the temples in the city had hosted candlelight processions, and many of the people lining the road carried candles. It wasn't hard to see how the Festival of Lights came by its name.

Cheers filled the air as Philippe's car passed, the royal standard fluttering in front. He waved and encouraged her to do the same. Feeling slightly fraudulent, she did so.

She was glad that Talay was celebrating the event with friends. The last thing Norah wanted was for the teenager to blurt out how Norah really felt about Philippe.

His temper hadn't improved by the time they reached the royal barge moored on the edge of Andaman Harbour. From here Philippe would launch the festivities.

He kept his feelings in check admirably, giving no outward sign of his black mood. When had she come to read him so well, she wondered? It made her sick at heart to be the cause of his displeasure, but there was nothing she could do to relieve it.

The air was fragrant with the scents of san-dalwood and joss sticks. Talay had told her that bonfires were being lit all over the city. Their glow gave the night sky a luminous look.

Despite the air of excitement, the festivities seemed endless to Norah. Did they seem so to Philippe? His regal bearing and set shoulders gave no clue as entertainers performed in an outdoor amphitheatre below them, followed by a spectacular fireworks display.

The moon was high by the time the festival reached its climax in the launching of the little boats. Each lotus-shaped craft was adorned with a lighted candle and flowers. In ancient times the ceremony had honoured the water spirits, and many people still thought the boats carried away bad luck.

An attendant handed Norah her boat, and she slipped into it the message of her heart's desire she had written earlier. The tears that had splashed onto it had since dried, but she caught her breath as she read her message of love one last time before setting the boat upon the water.

It was foolish superstition, but she felt her spirits lift as the boat joined the thousands of others upon the dark face of the harbour.

All over Sapphan, similar boats were being set adrift on every available body of water. Surely the combined power of so many hopes and dreams had to have some effect on the cosmos?

She straightened to the tumultuous cheers of the crowd. In the midst of the sound her ears registered a faint cracking noise, perhaps a delayed firework. But another part of her recognised what it was even as she saw Philippe's bodyguards spring into action.

Two of them plunged into the crowd towards the sound, while another thrust Philippe bodily across the barge. But he refused to be stopped, and barrelled past the bodyguard to put himself between Norah and the crowd.

There was another crack, and she felt the impact in her own body, thinking she had been shot, but the impact had come from Philippe slamming against her.

As she saw the gush of red from his shoulder she went cold from head to foot. 'Oh, God, Philippe. No, please . . .'

But the bodyguards surrounded Philippe, one of them buoying him away from her, although he tried to shrug the help aside. In moments he had been taken from the barge to his limousine. The banshee wail of its siren vibrated through her as the car sped off with its police escort.

She was in shock as Philippe's remaining staff helped her to another car, their bodies forming a screen around her. As she slumped against the seat she saw that the driver was Alec. Not only was he a familiar face, but he spoke English, thank Heaven. 'Where have they taken Philippe?' she demanded, aware of how close to hysteria she was. 'I must go to him.'

He shook his head. 'My orders are to get you to safety.'

She hammered on the car door, but they were already moving at speed. 'To hell with my safety. I must go to Philippe. If he hadn't tried to protect me . . .'

She almost broke then but held on by force of will. Philippe's bodyguards had already removed him from the line of fire. He had risked his life to protect her and been hurt. The sight of his blood stained her memory and reddened her vision. Looking down, she saw that her gown was peppered with red.

Her protests were to no avail. Neither was screaming, threatening or issuing orders in a cold, calm voice. Alec drove her to the palace and stood over her while she finished throwing possessions into her suitcase. She hadn't bothered to unpack it after the scene with Philippe, so it took only minutes.

'I can't leave without knowing he's all right,' she tried again. Alec had rocked her to her core with the news that Philippe had ordered her out of the country tonight. She had debated refusing to move, but Alec was quite capable of shifting her bodily. It seemed she had no choice but to leave, and it was shattering her heart into little pieces.

'Any news will be relayed to the airport before your flight,' Alec assured her. Being asked to pack off a shocked, semihysterical woman didn't faze him at all. He would obey Philippe's orders to the letter, no matter how bizarre-seeming.

'I'm supposed to be satisfied with that?' Alec didn't answer. 'I'll get off at the first stopover and catch a flight straight back here.'

A gleam very like admiration lit the fierce features. 'I will be at your side until you reach Australia.'

She tried another tack. 'Alec, please, I love Philippe. Don't take me away from him now, when he needs me.'

The rigid facade almost cracked, but he set his shoulders. 'I'm not the one asking, madam. The prince gave me the order himself. It's not up to me to question his wishes.'

Then maybe it was up to her. She handed Alec her case and followed him out of the suite. On the way to the car they passed the art gallery, where she hesitated. 'I left a book in here the other day. May I retrieve it?'

He nodded. 'I'll get it for you.'

'No, I . . . I know where it is. It will only take a second.'

She was back moments later, hoping he would think the nonexistent book was in her handbag. It wasn't. But she was carrying one of the priceless Naga carvings, like the one Jinny had tried to take out of the country only weeks—or was it days?— before. It felt like forever.

She had reckoned without Philippe's influence. Instead of passing through the usual security checkpoints, she was led to the head of the departure queue.

'Aren't they going to check my bags?' she asked Alec frantically.

'You are under the prince's patronage. It is not considered necessary.'

She stood her ground. 'I don't want any special privileges. The prince is ordering me out of the country. So I must be a desperate character.'

She had raised her voice deliberately and saw it was finally having an effect on Alec. 'Please stop,' he implored.

A senior security officer came forward. 'Is there a problem, madam?'

She shook off Alec's arm. 'I insist on being treated like everyone else or I won't board the plane.'

She saw him weigh up the alternatives and come to the least damaging one. 'Very well, madam, if you insist. But it really isn't necessary.'

'Oh, yes, it is.' Her heart sang as a very reluctant official began to give her things the most cursory inspection possible. He couldn't miss the Naga sitting prominently in her handbag, she'd made sure of it.

By now she knew enough Sapphanese to recognise the appalled conference he had with two other guards while Alec stood uncomfortably by. He knew, she thought, but there wasn't a thing he could do to stop the wheels of progress now. Was she imagining it, or did he look a little relieved?

With apologies she was shown to a VIP lounge and given coffee while she waited. While they worked out what to do with her, no doubt. She surveyed the pastel walls and soft leather furnishings. It was a far cry from the sterile security room at Chalong Airport where she'd been arrested and searched. In spite of herself she shuddered at the memory.

Would she be arrested again and held in the city until the palace could be contacted? Despite her

fear, she didn't care. She'd find the strength to
endure a night in gaol if it kept her in the country
until she knew that Philippe was all right.

The cup trembled in her hand, and she eyed it
dispassionately, as if it was held by someone else.
Shock was catching up with her, both from the as-
sassination attempt and from what she had done
to remain here. Would Philippe ever understand the
lengths her love had driven her to? She barely
understood it herself, only knowing that it was
stronger than anything she'd ever felt.

He didn't love her. Ejecting her from the country
proved it beyond doubt. He was even prepared to
risk constitutional mayhem to have the woman he
really wanted. That much was clear now. He must
feel as strongly about Kitma as Norah felt about
him.

His nearness to death tonight must have convinced him beyond doubt, prompting him to act
recklessly. Well, Norah was capable of reckless
action, too. Whether he loved her or not didn't
matter. She wasn't leaving Sapphan until she knew
he was out of danger.

A soft whimper escaped her throat. He could
have died. She set the cup down blindly and
dropped her face into her hands.

She didn't hear the door open until a resonant
voice spoke beside her. 'You seem to be making a
habit of this.'

That voice! She lifted her head but couldn't
speak. It *was* Philippe. She flung herself to her feet,

checking herself as she saw the sling supporting his left arm.

He caught her to him with his right arm, his concerned gaze taking in her face, which she knew was bone-white.

'It's all right, I'm here.'

She tried frantically to organise her thoughts. 'But how...why...'

'Isn't it what you wanted? Unless you're starting a collection of priceless antiques.'

The challenge in his voice grounded her. 'No, I'm not.' She sagged, and his strength buoyed her up. 'I know you want me to leave, but I had to know you were all right. Nothing else mattered.'

He sobered abruptly. 'I do want you to stay, but it wasn't safe. Until Alain was caught...'

Her eyes widened. 'Alain tried to shoot you?'

'Not me, darling, you.' The endearment almost went by her as she absorbed this new shock.

'Me? But why?'

'You're the one standing in the way of his ambitions. I glimpsed him in the crowd a second before the shots, and you were the one in his sights.'

But to try to kill her... Her knees weakened, and it was just as well for his strength. Now she understood why he had thrown off his guards and put himself between her and the crowd. He had known she was the target and risked his life to protect her. 'It's why you tried to hustle me out of the country, isn't it?'

His mouth twisted wryly. 'Without much success. When he awoke, Leon told me Alain was the one who sabotaged his call button. I gave orders for his arrest before the festival, but he lost himself in the crowds and stayed at large for some time after the attempt. Until he was caught, I didn't want you anywhere in his sights.'

Her numb brain finally made sense of his black mood before the festival. He'd known Alain was stalking her. Her anxiety flared anew, but for him this time. 'You're hurt. You shouldn't be here.'

He nodded. 'It's only a flesh wound, but the doctors won't be happy until I'm back in their clutches. But they didn't stand a chance once I was told what you'd pulled to stay here.'

He grew serious. 'Not even a bullet could stop me coming to the woman I love.'

She felt light-headed with confusion. 'Love? But you're in love with Kitma.'

'Another fiction created by Alain,' he stated. 'She and I are close, I admit it. In my position you have few confidantes, and you cherish those you have. Perhaps her brother mistook that closeness for love, or it was wishful thinking. Kitma is devastated by what Alain tried to do. By the time we return to the palace she'll have left the country for good. She knows I've loved you since the day I found you in my sculpture garden, half-dressed, wild-eyed, but with your own extraordinary beauty and dignity.'

'You accused me of leading my attacker on,' she reminded him in a husky whisper.

'Jealousy will make any man irrational, even a prince. I'd watched you all evening, hating every man who danced with you and especially hating

whoever had been out into the garden with you.'
He paused. 'It was Alain, wasn't it?'

She nodded. 'How did you guess?'

'It adds up. He knew how strongly I was attracted to you and set out to come between us from the first. Thank goodness it didn't work, or at least not for long. Can you forgive me?'

She pressed a finger to his lips. 'There's nothing to forgive. I've heard all I need to hear.'

Flames blazed in his eyes. 'Not even I love you?'

She sighed contentedly. 'I hear it even when you don't say it.' She looked at him with a glint of mischief. 'But say it anyway, as often as you like.'

'I love you,' he repeated obligingly, then went to take her arm but swore as the slight movement caused him obvious pain.

Her heart turned over. 'You must go back to the hospital and let them take care of you.'

He shook his head. 'We have something to do first.'

He wouldn't be dissuaded, and they were soon in his car, speeding through the darkened streets in a convoy of bemused police and staff. The airport staff had seemed relieved to see her go, and nothing more was said about the carving, which Alec had quietly retrieved for later return to the palace.

Now they stopped outside an imposing concrete and glass edifice framed by scaffolding. 'A building under construction? Why bring me here when you're in such pain?' He was not concealing from her his increasing suffering, which vibrated through her as if it was her own.

He dismissed it with a gesture. 'This is your building, Norah. I commissioned it for you.'

A tight band constricted around her chest. 'My clinic?'

'The first of many to be built for the Norah Rasada Foundation. I want you to be happy, no matter what it costs.' He took a deep breath. 'I'm even prepared to give up my throne and return with you to Australia, if it's what I must do to have you.'

Her eyes glittered. 'Not many women are offered a whole kingdom for love,' she said in a choked whisper. 'But I can't allow it. You belong here, Philippe. Your people need you, and I ... I need you, too. The clinic is wonderful, and I thank you from the bottom of my heart, but all I need to be happy is the knowledge that you love me and you intend to make me your wife.'

His mouth claimed hers in a passionate kiss, which left her breathless. When he lifted his head, his eyes were flame. 'Tonight you'll be my wife in every way. There will be no more doubts.'

Her body quivered with the need to know his total possession, but she touched the sling. 'What about your shoulder?'

He gave a throaty laugh. 'A man does not make love with his shoulder, my darling. Everything else is in perfect working order.'

Excitement coursed through her. 'You'll have to show me, Philippe.'

'Here, in the limousine?' He sounded seriously tempted. She wondered if she had even shocked him a little. If so, it wouldn't be the last time. He had

promised that he would rule Sapphan, but she
would rule him. All while using her womanly wiles
to avoid letting him know it, of course. What was
the saying? 'A man chases a woman until she
catches him.'

It was moot who had caught whom, but when
his arms enfolded her it didn't matter. Love was
for the heart, not the head, and her heart was
overflowing.

'Mummy, am I a king like Daddy?'

'No, Leon, you're the crown prince. One day far
in the future you will be king.'

'Will Malia be a king, too?'

'Princesses grow up to be queens, sweetheart. I
hope she'll fall in love with a handsome prince,
marry him and live happily ever after.'

'Like you and Daddy?'

'Yes, dear, just like us. Now go to sleep.'

'I forgot to ask God to bless you and Daddy and
Malia.'

'It's all right, Leon. He already did.'

MILLS & BOON®

Next Month's Romances

♡

Each month you can choose from a wide variety of romance novels from Mills & Boon. Below are the new titles to look out for next month from the Presents and Enchanted series.

Presents™

WICKED CAPRICE	Anne Mather
A LESSON IN SEDUCTION	Susan Napier
MADDIE'S LOVE-CHILD	Miranda Lee
A HUSBAND'S REVENGE	Lee Wilkinson
MARRIAGE-SHY	Karen van der Zee
HERS FOR A NIGHT	Kate Walker
A WIFE OF CONVENIENCE	Kim Lawrence
THE PLAYBOY	Catherine O'Connor

Enchanted™

LIVING NEXT DOOR TO ALEX	Catherine George
ENDING IN MARRIAGE	Debbie Macomber
SOPHIE'S SECRET	Anne Weale
VALENTINE, TEXAS	Kate Denton
THE BRIDE, THE BABY AND THE BEST MAN	Liz Fielding
A CONVENIENT BRIDE	Angela Wells
TO LASSO A LADY	Renee Roszel
TO LOVE THEM ALL	Eva Rutland

FREE!

FOUR FREE
specially selected
Enchanted™ novels
<u>PLUS</u> a Mystery Gift
when you return this card...

Return this coupon and we'll send you 4 Mills & Boon® Enchanted™ novels and a mystery gift absolutely FREE! We'll even pay the postage and packing for you.

We're making you this offer to introduce you to the benefits of the Reader Service™– FREE home delivery of brand-new Mills & Boon Enchanted novels, at least a month before they are available in the shops, FREE gifts and a monthly Newsletter packed with information.

Accepting these FREE books and gift places you under no obligation to buy, you may cancel at any time, even after receiving just your free shipment. Simply complete the coupon below and send it to:

MILLS & BOON READER SERVICE, FREEPOST, CROYDON, SURREY, CR9 3WZ.

No stamp needed

Yes, please send me 4 free Enchanted novels and a mystery gift. I understand that unless you hear from me, I will receive 6 superb new titles every month for just £2.10* each, postage and packing free. I am under no obligation to purchase any books and I may cancel or suspend my subscription at any time, but the free books and gift will be mine to keep in any case. (I am over 18 years of age)

N7XE

Ms/Mrs/Miss/Mr _____

Address _____

_____

_____ Postcode _____